'Miss Beaum[ont] [what are you] doing?'

'I'm avoiding someone, sir.'

'Avoiding someone?' Mark prompted easily, as though the incongruity of conversing with her in a musty office in the City rather than in an elegant drawing room in Mayfair had not occurred to him.

'Yes,' Emily breathed. 'The door was open and I just quickly darted in as I didn't want to speak to him any more.'

'If he's making a nuisance of himself I'm sure I can persuade him to desist.' As Mark drew level to her, a frisson of something akin to excitement jolted through her. The corridor was narrow and shadowy, and a musky sandalwood scent seemed to emanate from the warmth of his body.

Mark felt blood thicken his veins. He had an almost undeniable urge to trap her against the wall and kiss her senseless. She was the most unbelievably desirable little minx, even garbed in a voluminous cloak that disguised all her sweet curves. Miss Emily Beaumont might not like him, but he feared he might like her...a little too much...

AUTHOR NOTE

During the Regency period, genteel ladies hoping to find a husband were expected to be of impeccable reputation. In writing *The Hunter Brothers* duet of books, I have created heroines who don't quite fit Polite Society's view of an ideal wife.

In the first novel, A PRACTICAL MISTRESS, Sir Jason Hunter is captivated by a young widow brazen enough to proposition him.

The subsequent novel, THE WANTON BRIDE, features Mark Hunter, and his pursuit of a woman with a guilty secret in her past.

I hope you enjoy reading about two eligible gentlemen who are prepared to fight for the unique women they love.

THE WANTON
BRIDE

Mary Brendan

MILLS & BOON®

First published in Great Britain 2006
Paperback edition 2007
Harlequin Mills & Boon Limited,
Eton House, 18-24 Paradise Road, Richmond, Surrey TW9 1SR

© Mary Brendan 2006

ISBN-13: 978 0 263 85157 1
ISBN-10:   0 263 85157 5

Set in Times Roman 11¼ on 14¾ pt.
04-0207-59044

Printed and bound in Spain
by Litografia Rosés S.A., Barcelona

Mary Brendan was born in North London but now lives in rural Suffolk. She has always had a fascination with bygone days, and enjoys the research involved in writing historical fiction. When not at her word processor she can be found trying to bring order to a large overgrown garden, or browsing local fairs and junk shops for that elusive bargain.

Recent novels by the same author:

WEDDING NIGHT REVENGE*
THE UNKNOWN WIFE*
A SCANDALOUS MARRIAGE*
THE RAKE AND THE REBEL*
A PRACTICAL MISTRESS†

*The Meredith Sisters
†The Hunter Brothers

Chapter One

'Nonsense, my dear! There is nothing sinister in it. Boys like to go off gallivanting once in a while. You're worrying unnecessarily, I tell you!' Mr Cecil Beaumont gave his beautiful blonde daughter a beaming smile. 'Don't look so glum. He'll turn up when he's good and ready.'

'Tarquin is not a boy, Papa,' Emily Beaumont pointed out quietly. 'He is a man of twenty-seven and I suspect he has got himself into one scrape too many. Perhaps he has not succeeded in stalling his creditors and is in trouble.' Her silver-blue eyes took on a faraway look as she pondered on instances when her older brother had brought himself close to ruination through gaming and wild ways. But he had never yet disappeared for more than a few days before turning up, like the proverbial bad penny, sober and remorseful. 'Perhaps we ought to check with the authorities in case he is again in the Fleet.'

Mr Beaumont waved a dismissive hand. 'No need…no need, my dear.' He picked up his pen, idle on a page of his ledger, and set about using it.

His daughter was not so easily put off. Emily paced to the window of her father's den, stared out sightlessly, before wandering back into the room, deep in thought. With a sigh she sank into an old armchair.

Tarquin had been due to come to their parents' home in Callison Crescent and take their brother Robert to the outfitters. But he had failed to arrive at the appointed hour five days ago and had not contacted his family to make his excuses or his apologies. Emily thought it highly irregular behaviour, even for someone as self-centred as her brother.

Mrs Beaumont's reaction on that afternoon was to mutter about *the inconsiderate knave* before she got her husband's valet to take Robert to the tailors instead. When Emily had earlier today approached her mother about Tarquin's lengthy silence, she showed herself no more concerned over her eldest son's whereabouts than did her husband.

Mr Beaumont raised an indulgent paternal eye to

his daughter. He tossed his quill on to the blotter and clucked his tongue. 'Come, my dear, no long face, I beg you. If Tarquin had been threatened with prison, he would have by now summoned my help, you may take my word on it.' Cecil gave a cynical little laugh. 'I'll not go looking for him to sort out his troubles—if troubles he has—for they always find me soon enough.' A nod concluded his philosophy and he resumed his writing. A quiet moment passed. Warily he peeked up to find his daughter still in the room and looking no less melancholy. 'Emily!' he expostulated with a hint of impatience. 'If you're unable to put your mind at ease over it, I'll call in to Westbury Avenue and see if his landlady knows where he might be.'

Emily brightened. 'You promise you will do that, Papa?' she asked.

Cecil nodded affirmation. 'I can go that way to Boodle's later.'

A smile erased the strain from Emily's lovely features. Her father bowed his head over his ledger once more, gave a couple of short coughs, firmly letting Emily know their conversation was definitely concluded.

Emily rose gracefully from his armchair and went upstairs to her bedchamber.

Feeling lighter in spirits, she gazed out on to the street scene. She watched with an amount of amused interest as their neighbour's footman strutted back and forth on the pavement, trying to catch the eye of the housemaid scrubbing the front step of the house opposite. The young woman's complexion was as fiery as her hair and she looked too hot and bothered to presently entertain any thoughts of flirtation. Emily glanced up at a clear azure sky, then at fat green buds beginning to break on the lime trees guarding the crescent of townhouses. She decided she would call on her friend Sarah Harper who lived just a few turnings away. They could go for a stroll if Sarah was amenable to the idea of whiling away the afternoon with a chat and a browse in the shops. The day was clement and after a week of unremitting rain it would be nice to get out of the house and into the fresh air.

Emily was donning her coat by the front door when her mother appeared and frowned at her. 'You must take Millie with you if you are going abroad,' she lectured. 'That crone made a point of telling me that she recently saw you out without even a maid.'

Emily signalled her insouciance with a delicately arched eyebrow. She knew exactly to whom her mother was referring, for the two women were arch-enemies of long standing. 'Well, Mama, you must tell Violet Pearson that I am a woman of four and twenty and perfectly able to take care of myself.'

'Your age is not the point, and you know it,' Mrs Beaumont began, but her intention to furnish a lesson on etiquette and how it applied to spinsters came to nought. Her daughter gave her a little wave and skipped down the front steps. For a moment longer Penelope Beaumont stared at the front door. She shrugged—she was long used to her daughter's headstrong ways. It was just a nuisance when hags, with nothing better to do than cause trouble, sought to bring it to her attention. She turned about and headed towards the parlour and a fortifying nip of sherry.

'It *is* very odd behaviour,' Sarah commented and looked thoughtful. 'Surely your brother would at least pen a note to let you know if he is out of town.'

The two young ladies linked arms and promenaded towards Regent Street. They had decided to peruse the window displays of the new French *modiste* who had recently opened for business.

Sarah's frown lifted in tentative enlightenment. 'Perhaps Tarquin has fallen in love and has been lured to the country to do his courting.'

Emily chuckled. 'I'd like to think such a noble reason exists for his absence. Unfortunately, Tarquin is besotted with Lady Luck. No real woman could compete with such a possessive mistress.' She flashed Sarah a wry smile. 'I expect Papa is right and I am worrying needlessly. My thoughtless brother is probably just gone off on a revel with one of his chums. But it is bad of him not to say so and odd that he has let Robert down. He and Robert are friends, despite the age gap between them.' She frowned. 'It was not nice to see Robert's disappointment. He has gone back to school now and missed seeing Tarquin entirely.'

Emily's arm was given a tug as Sarah drew her towards Madame Joubert's shop. Behind small mullioned panes were draped a shimmering array of silks, artfully arranged to highlight their quality.

'The sea-green colour is divine…but the gold is an unusual shade.' Emily tilted her head to peer through the door. 'They have more inside…'

Sarah interrupted Emily's appreciation of the sumptuous cloths with a hissed, 'Look who is coming!' Emily's ribs received a dig. 'You ought ask *him* if he knows of Tarquin's whereabouts. They are friends after all.'

Emily glanced along the road and her eyes fixed

immediately on the man to whom Sarah had breathlessly referred. Indeed, it would be hard *not* to notice him. Mark Hunter was tall and broad with darkly attractive features that excited female attention. Emily recognised the elegant lady at his side who had her hand curved possessively over his arm. It was an open secret in polite society that Barbara Emerson was Mark Hunter's mistress.

'I see Mr Hunter has his *chère amie* with him,' Sarah whispered.

'I think it is more than *that* between them,' Emily returned on a little huff of laughter. 'I've heard a rumour that Mark Hunter is expected to marry Mrs Emerson. I imagine she considers herself to be his unofficial betrothed.'

Sarah arched an eyebrow. 'I wonder who started that rumour?' she said drily. 'And until *he* makes it official, there is still hope for us all. Goodness, he is handsome!' she breathed. 'I think I might swoon.'

Her friend's theatrical tone made Emily cast at her a small scowl. Sarah was quite aware that Emily did not like the man. 'Handsome is as handsome does…' Emily muttered in response to Sarah's teasing. Her eyes returned to the object of Sarah's admiration and lingered. Indisputably Mark Hunter *looked* a personable gentleman, but Emily had reason to believe him mean and callous. Was he not the fellow who had in the past had Tarquin imprisoned in the Fleet because he owed him money? Yet despite that betrayal her brother still liked Mark and classed him as one of his friends. On the few occasions Emily had quizzed him over his odd attachment to a man who had betrayed him, Tarquin had simply said Mark wasn't a bad fellow.

Emily pondered on Sarah's comment that this meeting might prove useful. Perhaps Tarquin's friend might know if he had recently gone off to Brighton or to the Newmarket races or some other such place where fashionable gentlemen chose to congregate. It was an opportunity to find out and she ought take it.

Her eyes flicked up as she realised that the distinguished couple were almost upon them.

'Miss Beaumont…Miss Harper.' Mark dipped his dark head and slowed his pace, allowing the young ladies time to respond. Sarah did so immediately. A shy smile accompanied her curtsy.

Emily sketched a bob and muttered his name. He was steadily watching her and boldly she met his eyes. They were an unusual shade of blue, she realised, not unlike the lustrous peacock silk she had moments ago admired in Madame Joubert's window.

A faint smile touched Mark's lips as he acknowledged her cool response and she glimpsed humour far back in his vivid eyes. Of course, he was aware that she didn't like him given that she had once frankly told him so. She hoped he was also aware that she found his good looks and ready charm quite resistible, even if her entranced friend did not. Emily shot a stern look at Sarah.

Aware that her lover seemed more interested in gazing at Emily Beaumont than conversing with her, Mrs Emerson quickly filled the silence. 'I have not seen you in a while, Miss Harper.' She turned to Sarah. 'How is your mother? When last we spoke she was afflicted with the rheumatics.'

'She is improved, I thank you, ma'am,' Sarah replied. 'When the weather is better, her condition is too.'

Barbara Emerson murmured her pleasure at knowing it, then turned to Emily. 'And you look very well, Miss Beaumont. Are your family in good health?'

Emily gave the elegant woman an affirmative and a fleeting smile. She guessed that Barbara Emerson was probably no more than a year or two older than was she, yet Barbara had an effortless air of sophistication that made her feel girlish in comparison.

Barbara had married a wealthy man at nineteen, been widowed and left his property and fortune at twenty-one and was now the mistress and aspirant future wife of one of society's most eligible bachelors. Emily charitably allowed that Barbara had earned her quietly superior attitude.

Noting that her attempt to distract her lover's attention from Miss Beaumont had failed, Barbara subtly urged Mark to move over the shop's threshold by squeezing the muscle beneath her fingers.

Emily felt Sarah's elbow nudge her side as wordlessly her friend reminded her to speak of Tarquin before the opportunity was lost.

Mark smoothly extricated his arm from Barbara's control in a way that was uncompromising yet courteous. With a faint flush livening her olive complexion, Barbara swished about and started to peruse the silks that had drawn Emily and Sarah to a halt by the window. Sarah stepped over to her and gamely indicated the colour she preferred.

'Is your brother at home, Miss Beaumont?'

'No, he went back to school this morning,' Emily immediately answered.

A wry smile tilted Mark's mouth. 'I meant your older brother,' he gently corrected.

'Oh…I thought you were referring to Robert—I

imagined you would know Tarquin is not with us.' Emily's small tongue stroked moisture to her dry lips. She felt faintly embarrassed by her gaffe, but her nervousness stemmed more from being constantly under his penetrating gaze. 'Actually, I was about to ask if you know where Tarquin might be.'

Mark frowned—he had discerned the quiver of anxiety in Emily's voice. 'I have not seen him since last week at White's when we played cards. I went this morning to his lodgings in Westbury Avenue, but his landlady said she'd not seen him for some days. I assumed he was staying with all of you at Callison Crescent. I'm not pursuing him for a gambling debt, I assure you,' Mark added mildly, noticing her sharp look. 'Tarquin expressed an interest in coming to Cambridge with me, that is all.'

Emily recalled then that Mark Hunter had a vast country estate in Cambridgeshire. Tarquin had visited it before and returned quite in awe of its size and splendid appointments. But now her thoughts returned to a place closer to home. She grimaced with disappointment as she recalled her conversation earlier with her father. 'Papa said he would call in at Westbury Avenue this afternoon. From what you have said, he will be wasting his time.' An unconscious sigh escaped Emily. 'It is too bad of Tarquin to go off like that without a word.' She raised anxious eyes to his face. 'Do you have any idea at all where he might be? I know he pursues unusual entertainment. Are there any boxing bouts or cockfights that might have taken him out of town?'

Mark looked down into a heart-shaped face that was tense with concern. She wanted his help and he would have loved to be able to give it. Unfortunately he had no idea where Tarquin was.

Despite knowing that Miss Emily Beaumont didn't like him, Mark had always harboured a soft spot for Tarquin's sister. It was not simply her looks that attracted him, although she was exquisitely pretty and had an alluring little figure. Presently her curves were primly hidden beneath her velvet coat, but he'd seen her dressed in less and admired the way her body tautened silk in all the right places. And on such occasions when she'd quickened his pulse, he'd brooded on trying to alter her opinion of him. Inwardly he smiled, for it would be no easy task. And therein lay another reason she held a fascination for him. Emily Beaumont had a robust character and was not too timid to challenge him or to speak her mind. A lamentable amount of young ladies tended to blush and stammer in his presence. Emily was more likely to flash him a glare from silver eyes than flirtatiously flutter those wonderfully long lashes at him.

But she was looking at him now in mute appeal and that surely indicated she was open to being persuaded he was not the heartless fellow she'd previously thought him. Mark was reasonably sure that her brother was simply lying low to avoid paying his dues. But he was willing to keep his thoughts to himself and act knightly for the beguiling chit.

'I've not heard of any such events taking place,' Mark said levelly. 'But that does not mean none exist. I can make some proper enquiries and try to find him, if you'd like me to,' he offered huskily.

Emily gave a spontaneous smile. 'Thank you, sir. I would indeed like you to do that. It would be reassuring to know that Tarquin is simply acting thoughtlessly and selfishly as usual.' She had, she realised with a pang of regret, betrayed criticism of her brother's character. Previously when with this man she had always been defensive if mention was made of Tarquin's shortcomings. But her patience was wearing thin where he was concerned. He had let them all down in the past with his antics and they had rallied to support and to protect him. But Tarquin gave little back—even in the way of thanks—and Emily was aware that her parents' lack of concern over his whereabouts sprang from a relief that their eldest son had taken himself and his problems away for a while.

Vexation caused a sigh to escape Emily. She would like to similarly forget Tarquin. Considering he had once driven away the only man she had ever loved, it seemed absurd that she could not banish the bothersome wretch from her mind.

Emily surfaced from her introspection to become conscious of a pair of deep blue eyes steadily watching her. Mark Hunter was aware of a momentary lapse in her role as loyal sibling. She guessed he was also reflecting on her reason for suddenly warming towards him.

Just minutes ago she had greeted Mark Hunter with distinct coolness. Now she felt awkward. They both knew that her abrupt change of attitude was simply due to the fact that she needed his help. That glint in his eyes was mockery, she was sure, and probably signalled that he thought her a hypocrite. And why should he not? She was on the verge of acknowledging it herself! Emily briskly dipped her head and took a step away from him.

'Were you about to go in and make some purchases?' Mark asked conversationally, seeking to delay her departure.

Emily shook her head. 'No…we were just window-shopping. If you do come across my brother, Mr Hunter, I'd be grateful if you'd remind him where the Beaumonts live. Perhaps he might think to call in and say hello. Good day, sir.'

A smile curved his lips, acknowledging her ironic tone. 'I won't forget, Miss Beaumont. I'll let you know if I discover Tarquin's likely whereabouts.'

After a murmur of gratitude Emily approached her friend and Mrs Emerson. Sarah was still persevering in trying to engage Barbara in a chat about French fashions. Barbara's responses had been limited to a variety of tight-lipped expressions.

After polite farewells Emily and Sarah walked off along Regent Street. They had distanced themselves by only a few yards when Sarah glanced back over a shoulder. 'He's still looking at you,' she hissed into Emily's small ear. 'And Mrs Emerson has an unladylike scowl on her face.'

'He could be looking at you,' Emily immediately pointed out. 'Barbara is probably in a fit of the sulks from having delayed her shopping spree. I don't say I blame her. Those silks looked quite wonderful. It is a shame we didn't see what else was on the shelves.'

'Let's go back,' Sarah breathed. 'Why should we not? We were at Madame Joubert's first, after all.'

'Don't be silly; it would look as though we're following them.' Emily gave Sarah's arm a little tug to turn her about. 'And stop staring at them, for goodness' sake!'

Chapter Two

'Stop staring at them, for Gawd's sake!'

The young woman's booted toe made ungentle contact with her companion's shin. He yelped and swore beneath his breath at her. 'Wot you do that fer, Jenny?' he snarled.

'To stop you gawping like an idiot,' Jenny Trent hissed back. 'This ain't the time and place to be seen.' The young woman shot a look from under dropped lids and cursed quietly. 'I reckon the nob she was talking to has spotted us watching her. We don't want to be tangling with the likes of him!'

Mickey Riley affected nonchalance as he turned to look across the street. Fleetingly he met Mark Hunter's steady stare. His attention soon returned to his companion. 'Fellow's looking at you, Jenny.' He leered at the pretty woman at his side. 'I know his sort. Quality with cash and an eye for petticoat, he is.' He chewed his lips and gave Jenny a sly look. 'We could've found richer pickings than Beaumont.'

'Bit late to be thinking that now!' She pinched his arm, urging him to move on. 'You and your daft ideas!' she scoffed.

Mickey Riley eyed the distinguished gentleman propped against the doorjamb of the posh shop, whose pretty ladybird was pointing out to him something she liked in the window. The fellow didn't seem that interested; he soon glanced again across the street. 'I reckon he's taken with you, Jen. Give him something to look at,' he urged his shapely young companion.

Jenny scowled up at Mickey, but did instinctively twitch at her skirts thus revealing a pair of shapely calves and ankles. She shook back her auburn curls, setting them bouncing beneath the elaborate concoction of feathers perched on her head.

'Good girl,' Mickey praised with an appreciative grin and threaded her arm through his.

Mark Hunter watched the couple disappear into the Regent Street throng. Had Mickey Riley known his thoughts, he might have felt less cocksure. It was not Jenny who had taken Mark's interest, but Mickey himself.

Mark allowed Barbara to steer him inside the shop. He made appropriate noises as she indicated the things she liked, but his thoughts were elsewhere.

It seemed a rather odd coincidence that Emily Beaumont should mention Tarquin and cockfights to him just moments before he clapped eyes on a fellow he had last seen arguing with Tarquin at a cockfight in Spitalfields Market. It had been a heated enough exchange for Mark to enquire after the fellow's identity. Tarquin had obliged him with that information when he subsequently joined him at the ringside of a boxing bout, but had seemed reluctant to divulge more about Mickey Riley, or the subject of their disagreement.

The incident had been some weeks ago, but Mark had a good memory for faces, and Riley's appearance was quite striking. He looked to be about Mark's own age of thirty-two, yet had hair as grey as smoke and a complexion that had been ravaged by the elements to nut brown. Riley also had a misshapen nose that led one to believe he was, or had once been, a pugilist. Notwithstanding those blemishes, he was well built, and an oddly handsome man.

When Mark had witnessed the altercation between Tarquin and Mickey—who was quite obviously of a different social class—he had not been surprised or concerned. Tarquin's love of gaming brought him into contact with all sorts of people at all sorts of venues. His friend would wager on a street scrap between two bruisers or a race of thoroughbreds at Epsom. Unfortunately, wherever he went, Tarquin had an unholy knack of backing a loser.

Most gentlemen with such an appalling record of luck would find diversion of a different kind. Yet after almost a decade, and a small fortune squandered, Tarquin still followed the philosophy that the next stake would bring it all right.

Mark's thoughts returned to Mickey Riley. If Tarquin owed him money—perhaps from a bet that night in Spitalfields—Riley didn't seem the sort of fellow to take the loss lightly. Of course, Tarquin's debts were not his business…at least, not until he decided to call in the loan he had made him last year, and added to them, Mark wryly reflected.

But the sardonic tilt to his lips was soon gone. Mark's mood became sombre, for he had an uneasy feeling that Mickey and his female companion had been watching Emily. Or it could have been Sarah Harper they were interested in, but instinct persuaded him it was not.

It seemed absurd to suppose that Riley might accost Emily because her brother owed him money.

But it was certainly not unheard of for even well-connected creditors to pursue the relatives of those who tried to renege on a deal. Big and brash as Riley looked, perhaps he was too craven to approach Mr Beaumont senior with his complaints and was stalking his daughter instead.

Mark darted impatient looks about the cloyingly scented shop. Madame Joubert was rustling hither and thither, her arms full of froth, as she tempted Barbara to make her purchases. As he watched the pretty trivia pile on the counter, he wondered whether he was letting his imagination run riot. There was little substance on which to found his suspicions.

He had no proof that Riley and his female companion were doing more than enjoying a leisurely afternoon stroll. If they had been watching Emily and her friend, was it necessarily from sinister motives? Two attractive young ladies, obviously of enviable status, were bound to draw the attention of those less privileged.

It was a reasonable explanation, but ultimately did not quell Mark's suspicions. He had a sudden urgent desire to quit the *modiste*'s, immediately track down Tarquin, and demand he tell him what the hell he had lately been up to.

* * *

'Man over there give it to me. He told me to bring it to you.'

Emily looked down at the ragged child who had moments ago yanked rudely on her coat to gain her attention. The boy had then stuck out a grimy hand that clutched a note. Tentatively Emily took the paper and then peered in the direction that the wizened-faced little urchin was pointing. She couldn't see anybody at all who looked to be the likely sender. People were stepping briskly along the pavements, going about their business with no hint of any interest in her.

She looked enquiringly at the boy, who was wrinkling his freckled nose. He cuffed at his face as he looked up and down the street. 'He's gorn,' he admitted with a shrug. 'But he was over there and he give me it and then he give me this.' Dirty fingers were opened to reveal a few coppers. 'You gonna give me anythin'?' he boldly asked and peered at Emily with one eye open and one closed against the afternoon sunlight brightening his sallow complexion.

Recovering her senses and her voice, Emily murmured, 'Oh, of course.' She fished in her reticule and then tipped a few more coins to chink on those reposing on his blackened palm. His fingers trapped the pennies, then he was haring away as though he feared she might snatch them back.

Emily walked on slowly towards Callison Crescent. She had a few minutes ago left Sarah at her door and had been barely five minutes from her own home when the lad had accosted her. Curiously she inspected the note. It was sealed, but there was no name or direction on it, just the sooty marks left by the child's fingers. She made to open it, then hesitated. With a little inner smile she wondered if perhaps she had a secret admirer. If so, she ought to, at her leisure, discover his identity. She slipped the parchment into a pocket. It certainly would not have come from the gentleman who openly admired her.

Mr Stephen Bond was not prone to such romantic gestures as employing guttersnipes to deliver her a billet-doux. But he was nice enough, if rather predictable. Emily let out a sigh. Thinking of that gentleman had reminded her that Mr Bond was due to dine with them later and of course he would be exceedingly punctual.

'I expected you home before this,' was the peevish greeting that Emily received from her mother as she stepped into the hallway. 'You have not forgot that we have company?'

'No, Mama,' Emily said. 'I know Mr Bond is coming at seven.'

'Well…good…let Millie do something pretty with your hair. The curls looks limp.' Her mother circled her and picked a loose golden tress from the shoulder of her blue velvet coat. 'Stephen is to bring his grandmamma with him this evening. She is up from Bath and seems eccentric. I was introduced to her at the Revue and couldn't but invite her when Stephen mentioned he was coming. She had on the ugliest gown I ever did see. It was a shade of purple with fawn stripes. What possessed her to wear a green hat with it?'

Emily gave her mother a wicked smile. 'If she arrives here in the same ensemble, perhaps we should demand to know.'

Penelope Beaumont chuckled, but her humour soon faded and she frowned at the door. 'And your father is late home too. It's nearly a quarter to six.'

'He said he would call in at Tarquin's lodgings. That has probably delayed him.'

'A man was looking for Tarquin.' Mrs Beaumont volunteered that information with a furrow in her brow. 'Millie ran an errand for me earlier and she said the fellow stopped her in the street. He must have watched her leaving the house or how would he know of a connection between them? She said he was polite to her despite seeming a bit of a rough sort.' Mrs Beaumont peered past her daughter as her husband entered the hallway brushing water from his caped shoulders. 'It's come on to rain again,' she gleefully remarked. 'The Pearsons will have to cancel their firework display.'

'It is as well then that you were not invited, Mama.' Emily was aware that her mother and Violet Pearson were continually sniping at one another. They had been at loggerheads since Robert planted a facer on Bertie, the Pearsons' son, thereby knocking out his two front teeth. The patresfamilias had shrugged and commiserated together about the young scamps. But Penelope Beaumont and Violet Pearson seemed determined to keep the feud alive.

'No sign of Tarquin, I'm afraid.' Mr Beaumont had deposited his damp coat on a chair and was wearily approaching the ladies. His tone had changed since that morning. Now Emily detected a distinct hint of anxiety making his voice husky.

'You went to Westbury Avenue, Papa?'

'I did, and Tarquin's landlady was pleased I had stopped off, I can tell you. I had no chance to ask her if she knew where he was. She demanded *I* disclose to *her* his direction. She is under the impression he has done a flit and will not be back.' Mr Beaumont sadly shook his head. 'Most of his possessions are gone and he owes her two months' rent. She has not seen hide nor hair of him for almost two weeks.'

'What are we to do with him?' Penelope Beaumont flapped her hands in exasperation. 'When will he settle himself down and act responsibly? I knew he was running away from his debts again.'

Cecil pursed his lips. 'In my opinion, it's more than the rent he owes that's bothering him. Mrs Dale told me a fellow with a broken nose had called at Westbury Avenue looking for him. She said he looked like a cove it would be best not to cross.'

Penelope Beaumont anxiously clasped her husband's arm. 'A man with a crooked nose stopped Millie in the street. He was asking about Tarquin. Millie said he seemed quite polite…' she added desperately.

'So he will be if he is about to demand his cash,' Mr Beaumont pointed out with a cynical grunt of a laugh. 'It's when he doesn't get it that he's likely to turn rude.'

Emily bit at her lip as she swung a glance between her parents' drawn countenances. Their brief respite from Tarquin's problems was at an end. He might still be out of sight, but imagining what sort of chaos he had created was tormenting their minds.

'I can't understand why he's not been in touch,' Mr Beaumont said. 'If he needs money, I'm usually his first port of call. I wonder if he's approached one of his friends to bail him out? I warned him last time that I'd do it no more. Mayhap he took me at my word.'

'I saw Mark Hunter when out,' Emily quickly volunteered that information. 'He also had called in at Westbury Avenue to look for Tarquin.' She immediately allayed her parents' fears as to why he would be seeking their son. 'It was not for payment of a debt, Mr Hunter assured me of that. He has not seen Tarquin recently either, but he kindly said he will make enquiries and let us know if he discovers anything.'

Cecil Beaumont nodded slowly. 'Mark is a good chap; if he says he will put himself out to do that, then I expect he will.' Cecil scraped lank greying locks off his freckled forehead. 'I suppose I ought open the post in case the bad news is come in a letter from Tarquin. Usually he just turns up and I can read it in his face.'

Emily's father trudged towards his study; her mother hurried away to check on their dinner. Before Penelope disappeared towards the kitchens, she called back to her daughter, 'Oh, for goodness' sake, make yourself presentable, Emily. Look at the time! The Bonds will be with us in less than an hour.'

As the baize door closed behind her agitated mother, Emily slowly slid her hand into her pocket. She withdrew the parchment and felt a chill settle about her heart. *Secret admirer, indeed!* she mocked herself.

She suddenly had a very strong suspicion as to who had sent her letter. The manner in which it had been delivered obviously indicated that her brother did not want her parents to know of its existence, or its content. But why had he not shown himself to her? Why had he sent the boy to deliver it? If he was too wary to approach her in the street, even for a few moments, then Emily realised he must be in bad trouble indeed. The paper was dropped back into her pocket and quickly Emily headed for the stairs and the privacy of her chamber.

'You are a pretty gel, but undoubtedly past your prime.'

Emily heard that ambiguous tribute as she was sipping her wine. She swallowed quickly, for an urge to giggle had caused her to almost choke. She coughed delicately while composing herself, then smiled at Mrs Augusta Bond. She deposited her glass back on the table.

'Emily is not yet five and twenty,' Mrs Beaumont stiffly interjected. 'Hardly in her dotage, I think.'

Augusta Bond raised her lorgnette and divided her myopic gaze between mother and daughter. 'Her chances of getting a husband are not so good as the younger gels out this year. Her looks come from her father's side,' the *grande dame* opined, then affected not to see the icy stare that comment elicited from her hostess. Augusta let her glasses fall against her ample bosom and resumed attacking her beef with her knife and fork.

Emily sensed the old harridan's grandson was looking her way. She knew Stephen would want to wordlessly convey his chagrin at his grandmother's shockingly blunt manner. Emily took pity on him and gave him a subtle smile. Immediately he returned her an apologetic grimace that caused his thick brows to disappear beneath his fringe of blonde curls.

'Miss Beaumont has an exceedingly fine singing voice,' Stephen nervously told his grandmother. When that praise failed to wring a compliment from the old lady, he added, 'And I've not encountered any young lady who can play the pianoforte so well, and without a piece of music to follow.'

'That don't mean she'll make a good wife,' Mrs Bond hissed at her grandson in an audible aside.

Emily quickly snatched up her glass and downed an unladylike quantity of wine in one gulp. Oddly she felt an urge to endorse Mrs Bond's advice to her grandson. Stephen Bond was a nice gentleman but, unless there was no option but to do it, she would not marry him. He deserved to be loved, not tolerated.

Emily's silver eyes, brimful of laughter, lifted to Stephen's embarrassed countenance, then darted to her mother's face. Penelope Beaumont's expression was a study of furious indignation.

Had Emily been in lighter spirits, she would have more fully appreciated the unexpected entertainment that had arrived punctually at seven o'clock in the stout shape of Mrs Augusta Bond. She might even have entered into the spirit of the game and given the mischievous old biddy a run for her money. But her eyes were drawn to where her papa sat quietly at the head of the table. He seemed to have withdrawn to a world of his own. Even his wife's frequent glares could not budge him from it.

Emily could guess what was preoccupying her poor papa. He was trying to fathom into what sort of trouble his eldest son had now plunged. Before dinner Emily had thought she would by now have an answer to that conundrum. But the letter she had received was not after all from her brother. However, it did concern him, and Emily was still pondering on the peculiar message she had received, and why it had come to her at all.

When Tarquin's creditors gathered, if they could not find him, they usually sought to inveigle her father into paying. But this time she had received the begging letter, albeit couched in covert terms.

A person who remained anonymous had issued her an invitation to meet them tomorrow by the pawnbrokers' shop in Whiting Street in order that she might learn something important concerning her brother. It also stated that she must keep the matter to herself to avoid a scandal.

Emily had marvelled at the audacity of the fellow. She had quickly concluded that the author must be one of Tarquin's creditors who hoped to coerce her to honour her brother's debt. She had also deduced that the likely culprit was the ruffian with the broken nose, who had been loitering about, because the message was poorly written.

Emily was not so naïve to believe that her brother gambled solely in the gentlemen's clubs with his peers, but the idea that he was consorting with a man sporting a broken nose and a lack of grammar was indeed disheartening. Nevertheless, she would keep the appointment, and she would keep it to herself. She glanced again at her father as he absently pushed food about on his plate. He was approaching his sixty-fifth birthday and had for too long been encumbered with Tarquin's problems. Emily had no intention of taking on the yoke and would make that abundantly clear to Tarquin as soon as she again got within earshot of the selfish wretch.

'Have you ever received a marriage proposal, Miss Beaumont?'

Emily focussed on the present and saw that Augusta Bond had her bright beady eyes on her.

'Has any man asked you to marry him?' the old lady insisted on knowing.

Emily glanced at her mother's hideously shocked expression. Stephen had ceased chewing in alarm and had one cheek bloated with food. Emily compressed her lips to suppress the giggle throbbing in her throat. She took a deep breath before replying calmly, 'Indeed I have, Mrs Bond. I was engaged when I was twenty.'

'Cry off, did he?'

'Umm…no. I think I did, actually,' Emily said and placed her napkin down on her plate.

'Emily was betrothed to Viscount Devlin.' Mrs Beaumont issued that information in a glacial tone.

The old lady raised her lorgnette and peered at Emily with a glimmer of respect. 'Managed to hook a title, did you? No chance of getting him back now he's married to the Corbett chit. I hear she's already increasing.'

'I'll see if the next course is ready,' Penelope enunciated frigidly and surged up majestically from the table.

Emily glanced at her father to see he was now very aware of the tension in the room. He was looking in concern at her as though fearing she was upset. She reassured him with a smile before sending a challenging look at Augusta.

The old lady's eyes narrowed behind the glass, but Emily had the oddest impression that, before she let fall her lorgnette, Augusta winked at her.

Chapter Three

'That woman is the rudest person I ever did meet!'

Emily had barely managed to put a foot over the threshold of the morning room when that exclamation assaulted her ears. She had hoped that a good night's sleep might dilute her mother's ire, but it seemed as strong as ever.

When their guests had left at ten of the clock last evening, Mrs Beaumont had needed several draughts of sherry and the ministrations of both her husband and daughter to calm her enough to get her to bed.

'And her grandson is so...*pleasant,* so...*inoffensive,*' Mrs Beaumont emphasised with a quivering finger. 'Do you think it is her age? She looks to have reached her three score years and ten. Perhaps she is becoming a little confused.'

'I think she knows exactly what she is about,' Emily said with a light chuckle. 'I imagine Mrs Bond likes to be shocking.'

Penelope Beaumont clucked disgust at that. She pushed the jam pot towards her daughter as Emily sat down opposite her at the breakfast table.

Emily commenced spreading blackberries on to her toast, saying, 'Mrs Bond might be getting on in years, but she seemed to me to be in robust health and, in an odd way, I quite liked her.'

When Penelope heard that, her chin sagged towards her bosom.

'Oh, come, Mama, you must admit Augusta has a certain lively spirit, and she plays a mean hand of piquet. Papa lost a crown to her.'

Penelope snapped together her lips. 'And that compensates for her insults? How dare she speak so! You are a beauty in your prime.'

'She said nothing that was not true.' Emily took a fond glance at her mother from under long brunette lashes. Penelope had long harboured hopes that a knight in shining armour would carry her only daughter off to his Mayfair mansion and a life of untold luxury. Emily's eyes shaded wistfully. The knave had tarried too long. Her mother was on the point of urging Emily to settle for Mr

Bond and a villa in Putney. Emily pushed away her plate and wiped crumbs from her slender fingers. 'You know I'm too old to successfully compete with the débutantes for a husband. And I do actually take after Papa's side of the family. The miniature of Grandmama Beaumont could be my likeness.'

'And what about Augusta's appalling insensitive remarks about your aborted betrothal?'

'She did not know of it, Mama, I'm sure. She simply asked if I had received any marriage proposals.'

'I'll wager she *did* know of it and was out to be provocative,' Penelope snorted in muted outrage. 'Dreadful woman! You might have again burst into tears over it all.'

'I have not burst into tears over it all for a long while,' Emily said softly. 'And I promise I will never do so again. As for Augusta, I think she genuinely knew nothing about it. She lives in the country and the scandal was not so great.' She paused before reciting, 'When Tarquin Beaumont gave Viscount Devlin a beating, thereby ruining his sister's chance of happiness with the Viscount, I imagine it got scant mention in Bath drawing rooms. The gossip in London lasted barely a week, thank heavens.'

'It was only so soon forgot because that hussy

Olivia Davidson ran off with her sister's husband and set all the cats' tongues wagging.'

'And how grateful I was for poor Miss Davidson's disgrace,' Emily reminisced wryly. 'I still feel a little guilty when I see Olivia's sour face,' she added.

'It's her own fault she's ostracised by everyone, including her own kin. Silly fool should have known he'd slink home with his tail between his legs and it would all end in tears.' Penelope flapped a hand. 'Oh, enough about them! We were talking of *your* fiasco. I still say you acted too proud and too hasty, Emily. You should have married the Viscount, you know.'

'Indeed?' Emily gave a sour little laugh. 'Nicholas had made it clear by then he regretted an association with our family. I had no intention of binding him to his word and having a husband who might grow to despise me.'

Penelope waved that away, but her further arguments were immediately interrupted.

'We have been through this before and I refuse to rake it all over again. It is done with.' The grit in Emily's tone was at odds with the easy smile she gave her mother. Gracefully she rose from the dining table and went to the window. 'I am going out early today. Madame Joubert has some fine new silk…'

'I'll come too. I need some buttons—'

'No.' Emily realised she had declined the offer of her mother's company far too abruptly. Penelope looked rather taken aback, so she hastened to say, 'I was going to find something nice for your birthday. It won't be a surprise if you come too.'

Penelope flushed in pleasure and murmured, 'Oh, I see…'

Emily felt a little guilty at the excuse, though she had not told a lie. She would call in to the *modiste*'s on Regent Street and would find her mama something special for her birthday. Nevertheless, her real reason for going early abroad this morning was to keep her rendezvous on Whiting Street with the person who had sent the note. And she had certainly no intention of letting her mother in on that.

Penelope Beaumont could become disproportionately agitated over a trifling upset. If a storm was about to break over Tarquin's debts, it would be prudent to shield her from the worst of it for as long as possible.

'Mr Bond is here, ma'am.' Millie had slipped into the room to announce they had a visitor.

Penelope frowned—it was hardly yet the hour to be receiving callers. She gave her daughter a quizzical look.

'I expect he has come to apologise for his grandmother's blunt manner.' Emily gestured that she had no objection to seeing him.

'We will receive him in the parlour, Millie,' Penelope told the young maidservant.

Once in the parlour, and in the company of their diffident guest, Mrs Beaumont proceeded to pour tea while Emily and Mr Bond made polite observations on the vagaries of spring weather. Stephen was handed his cup and saucer and accepted the invitation to sit down whereupon, without preamble, he set about doing his duty.

'I must apologise for calling on you so early but I wasn't sure…that is to say…' His eyes darted between the two ladies as though searching for assistance. He cleared his throat and blurted, 'I wanted to again thank you for such fine hospitality yesterday and to make sure that you had not…been perturbed by my grandmother's blunt manner.'

Stephen glanced at Penelope Beaumont. Something in her expression caused him to quickly add, 'My grandmother does not intend to upset people, but she can be rather too outspoken.' He took a gulp from his tea, then clattered the cup down to rest.

'Does she not understand that being too outspoken is likely to upset people?' Penelope asked stiffly.

Stephen coloured and coughed. 'I don't think she does, ma'am. But if you thought any of her remarks offensive I will, of course, unreservedly apologise on her behalf.'

Emily put her tea down on a side table and kindly said, 'I thought your grandmama was quite a character. I enjoyed meeting her.' Emily's smile turned wry as Stephen looked most surprised to hear that. 'If Mrs Bond is not soon returning to Bath, you must introduce her to Mrs Pearson.' Emily sent her mother a twinkling look. 'Do you not think, Mama, that Violet Pearson might benefit from an acquaintance with Stephen's grandmother?'

Finally that morning Emily had drawn a twitch of amusement from her mother.

'Do take another cup, Mr Bond,' Penelope urged amiably and advanced with the pot.

Emily checked the wall clock and stood up. She needed to be on her way if she was to keep her appointment. 'I'm going out shopping, but do stay and finish tea,' she added as Stephen leaped to his feet.

'I'll gladly give you a ride,' Stephen volunteered eagerly, raking his fingers through his springy blond curls. 'Actually I ought to be getting along too. I have an appointment in Holborn.'

'I accept your kind offer, in that case,' Emily said.

* * *

Despite his noticeably wonky nose, it was not the fellow's looks that drew Emily's attention, but his manner. He had the demeanour of a person oblivious to the fact that he was under observation. Back and forth he strutted beneath the brass balls of the pawnbroker's shop, every so often peering at the passing carts with obvious disappointment. Then, a few yards away, a hackney cab pulled up at the kerb. That sent the fellow darting into the shop doorway, only to reappear a moment later when a stout gentleman alighted from the vehicle and purposefully bowled off up the street.

Emily guessed he had been expecting to catch sight of her before she noticed him. Doubtless he imagined she would arrive at the pawnbroker's in a vehicle rather than on foot. But Emily had not wanted to be quizzed by Stephen over why she was to be set down in an area so lacking fashionable shops. Instead, she had asked him to deliver her to a salubrious part of town that was within easy striking distance of Whiting Street. Having first declined Stephen's offer to meet her later to take her home, she had then watched his rig turn the corner before briskly walking east.

It was a fine spring morning, but chilly gusts of

wind made her keep her cloak pulled tight about her. She again sent a discreet look across Whiting Street at the fellow she was sure had sent her the note.

Although his burly figure didn't intimidate her, she did feel nervous. This was an area generally populated by gentlemen. They came to these premises to meet their men of business and pore over contracts and unintelligible papers. A lone female loitering about was likely to incite curiosity. Emily knew that her own papa often had assignments on this street with his attorney. Fervently she prayed that he had not arranged a meeting with Mr Pritchard today.

'Emily? Emily Beaumont?'

That cultured voice, once so well known to her, made Emily freeze, then pivot slowly about.

Viscount Devlin had been about to get into a crested carriage, but now he hesitated and sauntered, with much use of his ebony cane, along the pavement towards her.

Emily had wondered how she would feel if ever she and this man were to meet, alone. Of course, since the end of their betrothal many years ago, they had met socially. But that had been in polite company when they both were mindful of etiquette and speculative stares.

Notwithstanding the fact that Emily knew the love of her life was now a husband and prospective father—for she had heard that his wife was increasing before Augusta mentioned it—she wondered if the Viscount's roguish charm would still impress her. The closer he came, the more she feared the potency of his attraction. He was still youthfully good looking and could have passed for a man half a decade younger than his thirty-one years. His fair hair was artfully dishevelled and his hazel eyes warm as they settled on her face.

'Are you waiting for your father?' he asked, surprise leavening his tone, as he took a glance along the street. Emily imagined he expected to spy Mr Beaumont emerging from a nearby portal.

'No…I'm not,' Emily answered too quickly and truthfully. She sought for an excuse for her odd presence on Whiting Street. But she need not have worried over any further interrogation from the Viscount—he now seemed distracted by her small tongue as it trailed moisture over her full pink lips.

Emily felt her heart begin to race beneath his languid appraisal. The heat smouldering in his eyes brought instantly to mind images of things they had done together that she thought she had buried deep in her past. A burst of knowledge brought with it a guilty exhilaration: Viscount Devlin still desired her.

'When was it that last we met?' the Viscount asked huskily, his tawny eyes moving to her body. 'It must have been a year ago. I swear that every time I see you, Emily, you have grown more lovely.'

Emily sensed her heart increase tempo, but flashed him a cool look from silver eyes. 'And I swear, sir, that I think you must be still recovering from a night of roistering to say such a thing to me.'

'Can I not compliment you?' he asked gravely. 'Why are you so prickly, Emily? Has the hurt not yet healed?'

Emily blinked. Part of her wanted to laugh scornfully at his terribly inappropriate remarks, but there was also a shameful part of her that would rather listen to more of his flattery. Mentally she shook herself and took a step away. He might tell her she was lovely, and look at her as though he wanted to kiss her, but her memory was not so short. A few years ago, after Tarquin had thrashed him, there had been nothing but disgust and anger in his eyes when he saw any Beaumont, including her.

'What you are referring to belongs to the past, sir,' she said stiltedly, 'and there is certainly nothing more to be said about it.' She bobbed and made to whip past him, but a hand shot out, arresting her.

'Don't fly away, Emily,' he softly pleaded. 'I have long thought that there *is* more to be said. I have wanted to see you alone; have hoped we might meet by chance like this. I think of you often. I think of what might have been…'

Emily twisted her wrist from his restraint and took two crisp backward steps. She darted a look here and there to see if they were under observation and was annoyed to notice that they were. The bruiser who had summoned her to this dratted neighbourhood in the first place had now spotted her! Emily frowned and sighed softly. The situation had become farcical. She was not now likely to discover Tarquin's whereabouts.

'Do you know him?' Viscount Devlin asked.

'Who?' Emily blurted and her eyes darted quickly to the Viscount's face.

'The fellow across the road who appears to be staring at you.'

Emily spontaneously shook her head. It was not a lie; she did not yet know him, but she was certain she had been within a few minutes of remedying that when Nicholas Devlin had turned up. In a way it was fortunate that the Viscount had come along when he did. A moment or two later and doubtless he would have seen her talking to the fellow and that would certainly have given rise to awkward questions.

Emily was aware that her brother and her erstwhile betrothed still shunned one another. Whereas Nicholas might show *her* a little sympathy and kindness, Tarquin would receive no such consideration. If her brother was again in bad trouble, she was certain that Nicholas would revel in knowing it.

Viscount Devlin shot a thoughtful look at Mickey Riley, for he knew the identity of the fellow, and how he made a living. In the past he had made use of his services for he had under his wing some extraordinarily pretty young women. Nicholas also knew that where Riley went, trouble usually followed. But he didn't fear him; in fact, he knew that Riley was cunning enough to keep a respectful distance between himself and his superiors. A smile twitched Nicholas's lips as he noticed that his steady regard was making Riley nervous. A moment later the man swaggered off along the street.

Emily watched the fellow departing too, realising quite miserably that her efforts to get here on time had been squandered. Her rendezvous was to come to nothing. She also realised, with a start of alarm, that Nicholas's expression had turned shrewd. She

guessed that he was about to interrogate her properly
as to her reasons for being here, unaccompanied, on
Whiting Street.

Quickly Emily shifted her gaze to an imposing
pillared doorway some yards to her right. She could
just decipher what was written on a bright brass
plaque: Woodgate and Wilson, Attorneys at Law.
The door was ajar and a sombre hallway could be
spotted within.

'I must be going or I shall be late for my appointment.' She gave Nicholas a brief nod.

'You have a meeting to keep?'

'Yes…with Mr Woodgate. It is a private matter.
Good day to you, sir.'

Emily turned and, with her skirts clutched in her
quivering fists, confidently went up the steps and
through the door that led, she imagined, to the of-
fices of Mr Woodgate and Mr Wilson. What she
would say to either of those gentlemen when they
begged leave to know why she was trespassing, she
had yet to decide. But at least she had put some distance between herself and the very disturbing presence of Viscount Devlin.

Nicholas watched Emily disappear, a smile thin-
ning his lips. Mickey Riley had been interested in
Emily Beaumont and she had been aware of him,

Nicholas was sure of it. In addition, Emily had been lying about having an appointment with Mr Woodgate. The practice dealt almost exclusively in marine law and insurance; besides, unless the lawyer had been disinterred for the occasion, she would not find Woodgate within that building. The man had been dead for some few months now. With a look of intense concentration drawing together his brows, the Viscount strolled back to his carriage and got in.

Sinking back into the hide squabs, he wondered what the devil was going on and decided his curiosity had been roused enough for him to make some investigations and try to find out.

Emily crept the musty corridor and ducked back from a doorway on glimpsing a young clerk scribbling in a ledger. His bony profile was just visible behind a pile of papers balanced on the edge of a desk. He must have caught her shadow, for he peered sideways into the corridor before resuming writing.

Emily loitered quietly in the hallway, her mind working furiously. If she were challenged, she would simply say that she had got lost and entered the wrong building. She would only need to tarry a short while for, once the Viscount had gone, she would make her escape. Inwardly she cursed. She had learned nothing today other than that the fellow with the broken nose, who had been loitering outside their house and making enquiries about Tarquin, *was* the sender of the note. He obviously had not liked being under scrutiny and had scampered off when it became clear that she and the Viscount had spotted him. Emily paced back and forth, wondering if she might manage to apprehend him and discover what on earth was going on. She silently went towards the door. If the coast were clear, she *would* try to catch up with the rogue.

'Miss Beaumont…what are you doing?'

Chapter Four

'**I**'m avoiding someone, sir.'

Despite the bizarre situation in which she found herself, Emily had spoken with admirably firm clarity. The only hint of her discomposure was in her unblinking, wide-eyed stare that clung to Mark Hunter's saturnine features.

He propped a negligent elbow on the wall as though prepared to wait for her to enlighten him further.

Emily slipped into a momentary daze that locked further explanation in her throat. His expression betrayed that he imagined she was stubbornly reticent, not tongue-tied. Obliquely she realised he must have emerged from one of the corridors that led off the main hallway. Mark Hunter obviously was a bona fide client of Messrs Woodgate and Wilson and had every right to be here to conduct his business.

'Avoiding someone?' Mark prompted easily, as though the incongruity of conversing with her in a musty office in the City rather than in an elegant drawing room in Mayfair had not occurred to him.

'Yes,' Emily breathed. 'The door was open and I just quickly darted in as I didn't want to speak to him any more.'

'If he's making a nuisance of himself, I'm sure I can persuade him to desist.' Mark had spoken quietly yet Emily sensed in him an alarming purposefulness. He came closer as though he would pass her and go to confront the fellow in the street.

'No! Thank you for your concern, but it is not that at all…' The thought that Viscount Devlin might be still loitering outside and faced being accused of bothering her made Emily's stomach churn queasily. As Mark drew level with her she grabbed hold of one of his arms to physically prevent him going out and causing a disturbance.

Barely had her small fingers curved over hard muscle when a *frisson* of something akin to excitement jolted through her. Suddenly she was very aware of how small and fragile she felt with Mark Hunter's tall, powerful frame looming over her. The corridor was narrow and shadowy and a musky sandalwood scent seemed to emanate from the warmth of his body.

Nicholas Devlin was a well-built man, but he had nothing like the height and breadth of Mark Hunter. Nicholas had different colouring too, being fair, not devilishly dark as was this gentleman. Emily's eyes levelled on a powerful shoulder clad in excellent grey superfine before slowly raising to a lean, angular face. Her breath caught in her throat as his gaze became sleepy and settled on her parted mouth.

Mark felt blood thicken his veins. He had an almost undeniable urge to trap her against the wall and kiss her senseless. She was the most unbelievably desirable little minx, even garbed in a voluminous cloak that disguised all her sweet curves. The distinctly wary look she was giving him did nothing to subdue the throb in his loins. Miss Emily Beaumont might not like him, but he feared he might like her… a little too much…

A dry cough shattered the tension and made Emily snatch her hand from Mark's sleeve and spring back from him like a scalded cat.

'Is everything in order, Mr Hunter?' The voice was nasal and insinuating.

Emily darted a sideways look at the gentleman

who was peering over the rim of his spectacles at them. He was of middle years and was wearing sombre clothes and a grim expression. His lids descended low over eyes brimming with disgust directed at Emily.

'I assure you this lady is not a client of mine, Mr Hunter. I'll send for a runner and have her immediately ejected if she is troubling you…'

'She is not,' Mark enunciated very coolly, very quietly. 'She is a friend and I am taking her home.'

Emily felt blood flood her face. The lawyer—for she guessed that was who he was—thought she was… Shock and outrage vied for precedence. The infernal cheek of the man! It was true she was not supposed to be here. It was also true he had come upon them when she had hold of Mark Hunter and their bodies had been pressed close together in a gloomy corridor, but… Emily's fury started to fade. The bald facts, so examined, did hint that a dalliance might have been taking place. That thought caused a fresh surge of colour to brighten her pale cheeks.

Mr Wilson now looked no less embarrassed than did Emily. He shuffled on the spot and mumbled an incoherent apology while pulling and pushing his spectacles back and forth on his hooked nose. Suddenly he slipped back out of sight through a doorway. He had made his escape at the right time; Emily's indignation had rekindled and she had been considering dodging past Mark so that she might go and remonstrate with the pious busybody.

As though sensing belligerence was keeping her small frame tight as a spring, Mark turned her firmly about and, taking her by the elbow, propelled her back out into the sunlight and down the steps. He glanced up and down the street. There was nobody loitering in the vicinity.

'Your troublesome fellow seems to have gone. Who was it?' he asked easily. 'An acquaintance…a stranger?' He raised a hand to signal and an impressively smart curricle drew to a stop at the kerb. The tiger nimbly disembarked and held the reins for his master, awaiting instruction to take his position at the rear of the vehicle.

Emily quickly took a step away from him, her mind in turmoil. She had set out this morning with just her brother creating havoc in her thoughts. Now two other gentlemen were also disturbing her peace of mind, and for the same reason: this afternoon both had wanted to kiss her, she was sure of it.

A short while ago Viscount Devlin had made no secret of the fact that he found her attractive: he had openly told her so. Nothing that could be construed as flattery had passed Mark Hunter's lips, yet she knew that just moments ago he also had looked at her with lust in his eyes. The lawyer would have been more justified in directing his scruples at his client than at her! Heavens above! She didn't even like Mark Hunter, let alone want him to kiss her… Emily frowned at her shoes; an odd fluttery feeling had revived in her as she recalled the sensation of their bodies touching in the corridor.

Mark watched flitting emotions animating Emily's sweet features. He guessed that the lawyer's assumption that she had been a soliciting harlot still disturbed her. She had every right to her indignation. The man had made a crass remark and deserved a reprimand.

'Mr Wilson is a cynic and a fool to have supposed a lady of your beauty and stature might be up to no good. All I can say in his defence is that the poor light must have prevented him getting a proper look at you.' Mark paused, aware that mentioning the incident had caused her fiery embarrassment. Gently he added, 'I will admit he is a fellow not much acquainted with charitable thoughts. But he is an excellent lawyer. Do you want me to fetch him so he might properly apologise?'

Emily looked up into eyes that were warm and rueful. 'You would do that?'

'Of course,' Mark said and stepped away from her. He came close again. 'But only if you promise to wait here until I return so I might take you home.'

The idea of again being trapped in close confinement with Mark Hunter, this time in his vehicle, made Emily blurt, 'Thank you for the kind offer, sir, but there is no need for you to trouble yourself. I can hail a cab.'

Mark casually repositioned himself and in doing so blocked Emily's retreat. She halted abruptly to avoid bumping into him.

'I hope you are not going to make of me a liar, Miss Beaumont.' Mark's tone was mock-grave. 'Mr Wilson is even now spying on us to see if we *are* friends and I *do* take you home.'

Emily glanced quickly at the building and immediately noticed a blind dropping back into place at a square-paned window. Renewed mortification sent heat fizzing beneath her cheeks. 'Insufferable man,' she muttered.

'I take it that was directed at Mr Wilson, not at me,' Mark drily remarked.

Emily looked up at him through a web of lashes and reluctantly returned him a small smile.

'Shall I reprimand him before we leave?'

Emily shook her head, setting her blonde tresses

dancing beneath her bonnet. 'No; it was not entirely his fault that he mistook the situation. What he saw must have looked…odd…' She bit her lip and frowned across the street.

Mark held out a hand to her and she permitted him to help her aboard his curricle. 'Genteel young ladies are not often seen alone in these parts. They come usually with their male relations if they have business to conduct.'

That seemed to Emily to be a purposeful observation. She guessed he might next enquire what her business had been coming here in the first place. Keen to continue an easy dialogue, she quickly said, 'I expect Mr Woodgate is nicer than Mr Wilson. It *was* Mr Wilson who appeared, was it not?'

'Indeed it was.' Mark set the beautiful greys in motion and drew smoothly into the flow of traffic in the street. 'Mr Woodgate was a very decent chap. Mr Wilson was a better fellow too before his partner died. I think he now finds it all too much to deal with alone.'

'Died?' Emily echoed, aghast.

'Mr Woodgate died suddenly of a heart attack some months ago now.'

Emily inwardly cursed that she'd made a mistake. Obviously Nicholas Devlin would have known that

Woodgate was dead. It piqued Emily that her erstwhile fiancé knew she had lied about an appointment simply to dodge into the building and get away from him.

'Are you not going to tell me who you were hiding from? Is his identity a secret?'

It seemed Mark Hunter's thoughts were in tune with hers so Emily sought a brief explanation. 'He is just an acquaintance; a gentleman I have not seen or spoken to for some while.' To prevent a further interrogation she continued, 'I have to purchase a birthday present for my mother. Would you be good enough to set me down in Regent's Street? I should like to go to Madame Joubert's.'

Mention of the *modiste* brought to mind the last time they had met. On that occasion Sarah had been with her when Mark and his mistress had chanced upon them window-shopping. Mark had volunteered to try to discover Tarquin's whereabouts while Sarah and Barbara Emerson had looked at the silks. Quizzing Mark now over her brother might yield some information about Tarquin and have the added benefit of distracting him from questioning her further about Nicholas. Emily frowned at her hands for, in truth, she had no idea why she did not want Mark Hunter to know she had been avoiding the man who had come within a hair's breadth of being her husband.

'We have still not had word from Tarquin. Have you discovered anything that might shed light on what he is up to?' Emily's eyes shadowed as she recalled her parents' anxiety over the lengthy silence from their eldest son. 'My father is now quite concerned about him. Tarquin usually contacts him if he has problems, and we are sure he has. His landlady has not seen him for weeks and he appears to have left without paying his rent.'

Mark reined in the greys and glanced at Emily's profile. She was chewing at her soft lower lip and slender fingers were intertwining nervously in her lap. Suddenly she turned and shot up at him a look of pure entreaty.

Mark felt the tightening in his gut that was not solely a lustful reaction to her sweet appeal. Emily Beaumont was getting under his skin in a way that disturbed him. In the hallway of the lawyer's office he had been on the point of kissing her when they were interrupted. In truth, he was sorely tempted to divert to a quiet spot and do it now…but equally he wanted to find Tarquin and bawl him out for putting her through such torment. Mark's jaw tightened as a liquid silver gaze clung to him. He snapped his eyes to the road ahead.

He had an idea where Tarquin might be hiding out, and he had discovered a bit about what the miscreant had recently been up to before he dropped from sight. It was not the sort of thing that could be recounted to the man's unmarried sister.

Mark's brother had volunteered some information when asked whether he had seen Tarquin recently. Sir Jason Hunter and his wife, Helen, had been returning from a performance in Drury Lane when they had spotted Tarquin drunkenly consorting with low life in a dark alleyway. Jason had drolly recounted how a particularly comely harlot had seemed to have a tenacious grip on his affections.

A grim smile twitched Mark's lips. Perhaps Tarquin had taken seriously the sarcastic advice he had given him some months ago and was sampling a variety of vices instead of expending all his resources solely on gambling.

Emily's soulful eyes were still on him and she was waiting patiently for his answer. Carefully he told her the bare bones of what he knew. 'My brother and sister-in-law saw Tarquin about two weeks ago. I promise I will continue to investigate.'

'Where was that? Where did they see him?' Emily demanded to know. Mentally she made a note to call on Lady Hunter. Helen and she had been friends since before Helen's marriage to Sir Jason Hunter.

'They spotted him in the Covent Garden area when they were returning from the opera.'

'Was he at the theatre too?' Emily asked quickly. 'Who was he with? We might be able to extract more information from his companions,' she said excitedly.

'He wasn't in the theatre and his companions, from their description, will be hard to find. Jason only caught a glimpse of him from his carriage when journeying home. I promise I will find your brother,' Mark said huskily as he drew the curricle to a halt outside Madame Joubert's.

Emily held Mark's gaze and in her mind whirled conflicting thoughts. Part of her was tempted to divulge to Mark that she had a little information on her brother too. Should she tell him that she had received a letter summoning her to Whiting Street? Mark might recognise the description of the fellow with the broken nose and be able to shed some light on his identity, and how he might be connected to Tarquin. But Emily's natural caution with this man kept the words hovering on her tongue tip.

Mark Hunter had once had her brother sent to gaol over a paltry debt of a hundred pounds. They were friends again, but how dedicated was Mark

Hunter to helping Tarquin? Emily didn't really trust him or his loyalty to her brother.

Earlier she had reflected on the differences between Mark Hunter and Nicholas Devlin, but they had at least one thing in common: both had a keener interest in her than in her brother. And it was an interest she had no intention of encouraging. Both gentlemen were spoken for; yet today she had had first-hand knowledge of how fickle-hearted they were as husbands and lovers. With just a little encouragement—and a little privacy—she could have been kissed by either of them. The fact that they both were firmly attached elsewhere, yet would like to engage in a little dalliance with her made Emily seethe with indignation. Perhaps they imagined that, as she had reached an age when it was considered she might be left on the shelf, she would be grateful for their lecherous attention.

'I'll wait for you to make your purchases and take you home.'

Emily allowed the young tiger to help her dismount. Yes, indeed, Mark Hunter was definitely showing her a little more consideration than was due to the sister of one of his friends. He was angling, she was sure, to seduce her, and doubtless he thought his good looks and affluence would make her fall into his arms. Perhaps he imagined that she was so desperate for his help in finding Tarquin that she might act like a gullible fool. But she had acted so once before, with Nicholas, and had vowed never to do so again.

The Hunter brothers had long been known as rakish characters. Jason had reformed when he married Helen Marlowe and was now a devoted husband. Acidly Emily wondered whether Mark would similarly change when Mrs Emerson finally got him to the altar.

Subduing a sour smile, she swung about to look up at him from the pavement. He returned her gaze with a steady intensity that confirmed her suspicions. He wanted her.

'Thank you for the ride, sir,' Emily began lightly, 'and for the offer to wait, but I have other things to do besides shopping.' Before entering the *modiste*'s, she hesitated, beset by an urge to turn her head and see if he was still watching her.

Slowly she pivoted around and noticed that the curricle was quite still and so was he. Their eyes tangled for a moment, then Emily looked away. Her mind foraged for something to say to explain away her reason for stopping to stare at him. 'Of course, if you learn any more about Tarquin's dealings, then, good or bad, we would welcome news of him.' Without waiting for his reply, she quickly whisked about and entered the shop.

Chapter Five

'**W**hat did she say?'

Jenny Trent's excited query drew nothing but a dark scowl from Mickey Riley. A sulky shrug slipped her hand from his shoulder and he slumped down on to a threadbare sofa. A stove was burning in the cramped back parlour they rented, but washing draped over a chair was blocking its meagre heat. Belligerently Mickey kicked away the obstruction and it overturned scattering the clothes onto grimy floorboards.

'This place is a dump. Don't you ever clean up, woman?'

Jenny slid a wary glance at Mickey as she put the chair back on its rickety legs. She picked up her stockings and petticoats, giving them a shake, before neatly arranging them on the slats again so they might dry.

'She won't fall fer it, will she?' she said as she hung the last scrap of linen on black oak.

'Dunno yet,' Riley snapped.

Jenny eyed Mickey's surly features, then perched on a stool opposite him. 'She didn't turn up,' she muttered scornfully. 'I told you it would be a waste of time.'

Mickey Riley surged to his feet, fists balled at his side. 'I did right, I tell you,' he bawled. 'She was there, and on time, but an accursed nob went up to her. Then he saw me, and looked a bit curious, so I didn't hang around. I know him. You do too. It was Devlin and I ain't getting on his wrong side.'

'Devlin?' Jenny echoed, startled. Oh, she knew *him* and hated it when she caught his attention and he chose to spend cash on her. That fine and dandy appearance of his hid a nasty rough streak. 'Do you think Tarquin's sister told Devlin about the letter you sent?'

Mickey shook his head. 'When he clocked me I walked off, but not far. I watched them from an alley. They was only together a few minutes. Looked to me like she was keen to dodge him 'n' all. She nipped in Wilson's office and Devlin went off in his carriage.'

'Did you wait for her to come out?'

Mickey nodded and grunted a laugh. 'Waste of time it were, too. When she came out of Wilson's she was with another fellow. It were the same swell she was talking to by the posh French shop. She must've liked him good 'nuff—she went off with him in his flash rig. And that were the end of me chances.'

Jenny chewed her lower lip pensively. For a few moments the tiny room was quiet except for the sound of her tapping her small booted feet in rhythm against the dirty bare boards. 'You gonna try fer another chance to meet her?' she suddenly piped up.

Mickey's curt nod answered her.

'Won't do no good.' Her derision was emphasised by an impatient hand flick. 'We ain't never gonna find Tarquin like this. We should forget him and find another punter.'

A string of curses from Mickey met that suggestion.

Jenny more volubly repeated her idea.

'Hold your tongue, woman,' he roared. 'Can't you see I'm thinking?'

'Penny for your thoughts…'

Mark surfaced from his sightless contemplation of the ceiling as his naked mistress leaned over him and kissed him on the lips. A corner of his mouth tilted in appreciation, but his hands remained pillowing his head, his blue eyes watching the spectral shadows above him.

'What are you thinking about?' Barbara asked huskily, stretching out sinuously on the feather mattress beside him. She slid a finger softly over the muscled ridges on his torso, then let it drift lower. Her tone had hinted at pique, but she was canny enough not to vent it. For some weeks now she had sensed that her hold on this charismatic bachelor was weakening. She didn't want that; she wanted his ring on her finger and her belly swelling with his child. After many years together as friends and lovers she wanted a promotion in Mark Hunter's life.

They were of similar age and a decade ago had been planning to marry, although no formal arrangements were made. Then Mark had taken himself off on a Grand Tour despite Barbara's protestations. Barbara had been desolate to discover that he was not after all crooked as tightly about her finger as she would have liked. It was shortly after Mark sailed for France that she, while still in a temper, accepted a proposal from someone much older and far richer. She had long regretted resorting to such tactics to punish Mark for abandoning her.

On his return to England, Mark had seemed insultingly philosophical over his loss. Barbara had been wounded to the core by his attitude—simply imagining his foreign *amours* made her jealous. But they had again become lovers when her husband died.

Not so long ago she could inflame him with a touch, a kiss, into passionate hour-long lovemaking. Now she had to work at wooing him. Her fingers fanned on his firm flesh in strong, sensual massage and she leaned close, seductively swaying her breasts against his chest.

Absently Mark tasted her eager lips and a hand cupped behind her raven head. He allowed her to arouse him, quite selfishly, for some minutes while the haunting image of blonde hair and silver-blue eyes danced erotically behind his lids. With a low curse he banished the tantalising images of Miss Beaumont and, turning swiftly, paid attention to the woman he was with.

Mark Hunter was not the only gentleman behaving with a distinct lack of gallantry because Emily had captivated his mind.

Barely ten minutes after arriving in his wife's bedchamber, Viscount Devlin shrugged into his silk dressing gown and strolled out again. If he was aware of the Viscountess's glittering eyes watching him, he gave no sign that her frustration and sadness bothered him.

He had married her five months ago and got her with child almost immediately. He had also just claimed his conjugal rights but was, as usual, left unsatisfied. Instead of heading towards the four-poster in his chamber, he strolled to the large window that overlooked Cleveland Street. Nicholas gazed into the night sky and brooded on the woman he knew certainly could extinguish the fire in his loins.

It was not that he wished he had married Emily Beaumont. He had a wife who was infinitely more suited to the role. Frances was attractive, placid and amenable. Most importantly, she had brought with her an enormous dowry and impressive family connections.

Emily had none of those material advantages. But she was beautiful and, as he had discovered to his delight, passionately responsive. In Nicholas's opinion, Emily Beaumont, but for an accident of gentle birth, would have made a most exquisite courtesan. She had a natural vivacity tempered with shyness; she had the body of a sensual goddess but was engagingly innocent. When he had met her at Al-mack's, she had been an entrancing mix of child and woman and he had wanted her—desperately. Thus the urge to propose to her had come from his loins, not his heart, and virtually as soon as it was done he had been cursing himself for an impetuous fool.

From the start he had known that she would not allow herself to be seduced by a man who did not love her or want to marry her. So he had told her what he knew she longed to hear and mercilessly fostered her devotion to him. With her father, he had spoken of honour and security and sounded noble and sincere.

But he was cursed with the Devlin trait of profligacy, as had been his father before him. As his spending continued apace and his bank balance sank to an alarming level, he had wondered constantly how he might extricate himself to hunt a fortune without bringing opprobrium down on his head.

Fortuitously Tarquin Beaumont had saved him the bother of pondering long on devious tactics. He had not forgiven Tarquin for that beating, but their enmity had served a very useful purpose and set him free to stalk an heiress. And now, with his wife increasingly fat and boring, possessing Emily again was becoming an obsession.

When he had told Emily this afternoon that he had been thinking of her, he had spoken the truth. For months past she had constantly been in his mind. He rarely saw her, for socially they moved in different circles. The opportunity to meet her alone had seemed just yesterday a hopeless ambition. But today it had come about. She might act coolly towards him, but he could tell she was not indifferent. Emily was older, more worldly-wise and, with a little subtlety, he was confident he could seduce her again.

Now that his wife had brought him such riches, he didn't see why he should not slake his lust with a woman of refinement rather than Mickey Riley's sluts. He had the wherewithal to set up a mistress in style in a fashionable part of town. And he knew exactly whom he wanted to visit. All he had to do was get Emily to accept his proposition…

Nicholas smiled at the twinkling stars; perhaps discovering why Emily had been acting so deviously in Whiting Street, with Mickey Riley watching her, might help bring it all about.

'Emily!' Helen Hunter rose from the chair and rushed to greet her visitor. 'How good to see you. My! You're an early bird!'

Emily embraced her friend and accepted the offer to be seated in Lady Hunter's elegantly furnished rose salon. With a little grimace she said, 'I know it's quite unfashionable to be out of doors at this hour, but I have something pressing I need to ask you.'

Helen scooped up from her seat the journal she had moments before been reading and dropped it to the carpet. She sat down and gave her friend an enquiring smile. 'Well, now, I'm intrigued as well as pleased by your visit. Please ask away without delay.'

Emily bit her lip, then blurted, 'I saw your brother-in-law yesterday and I wanted to quiz you over something he said.'

Helen settled back into her armchair with a wry expression. She knew very well that Emily did not like Mark, and why that was. She also knew from her husband, Jason, that Mark's motives for having Emily's brother imprisoned had been altruistic rather than spiteful. 'Has Mark said something to upset you?' It was doubtfully suggested—Helen knew that her brother-in-law went out of his way to be pleasant with Emily. In fact, she had a strong suspicion that Mark liked Emily and was quite hurt that she felt so differently towards him.

'No, he has not upset me…not intentionally, in any case. Mark told me something about Tarquin. Well, in truth, I rather prised the information from him.'

Helen chuckled. 'Would you care to start again?'

Emily gestured apology for the garbled explanation and, with a sigh, removed her bonnet and gloves and settled back to gather her thoughts.

'Let's have some tea,' Helen suggested. 'If we are to get our teeth into something—and I rather think we are—we shall need some refreshment.'

Helen Hunter and Emily were close friends who had over the years confided secrets both good and bad. In fact, just two weeks ago, Emily had been entrusted with the wonderful news, before it was officially out, that Helen suspected she was expecting her first-born. Thus, between sips of tea, Helen had no qualms in directly answering Emily's questions about when last she had seen Tarquin. She told her friend that she had witnessed him embracing a hussy in an alley close to Covent Garden. Helen was then surprised to learn that Tarquin had, afterwards, seemed to have disappeared.

Following that first burst of vital dialogue, the two young ladies sat in pensive silence for a few minutes and finished their tea.

Emily suddenly deposited her cup, in a clatter, on a side table. 'Tell me honestly, Helen…do you think he has been set about? Are you thinking, as I am, that these…these rough people might have robbed Tarquin? Beaten him? They might not have meant to do him real harm but…do you think a terrible accident might have occurred? Oh, where *is* the wretch?'

Helen jumped to her feet and flew to Emily's

chair. 'Hush,' she soothed, crouching down to comfort her friend. 'It is surely not the case. If every gentleman who consorted with a Covent Garden nun was attacked and disappeared, Almack's would be sadly bereft of bachelors on a Wednesday evening.'

Emily managed a chuckle at that wry observation. 'Do you suppose he is simply still on a drunken revel?'

Helen elevated her dark brows. 'If he is, he *will* return with a sore head, beating or no beating.' Helen took Emily's agitated fingers into her own. 'Shall I ask Jason to try to find him?'

Emily vigorously shook her head. 'Mark has already offered to make some investigations. I would not put Sir Jason to the bother of it too.' Suddenly a look of enlightenment lifted her features. 'I wonder if that is why the ruffian with the wonky nose sent me the letter: to tell me he knows Tarquin is unwell and cannot get home. It might not be about a gambling debt at all, but I expect he will, in any case, want some money for his trouble…'

Helen's astonished laugh curtailed Emily's further ramblings. 'I think you must immediately explain some more. Letter? Ruffian with a wonky nose? What *is* going on?'

'That is what *I* should like to know,' Emily returned pithily. But she went on quickly to explain all about her fruitless trip to Whiting Street and that she had had the bad luck to meet both Viscount Devlin and Mark Hunter there.

As Emily would have rushed on, Helen put up a silencing hand. 'Wait a moment. I must know more of this. You have been talking to the man to whom you were engaged? I thought you and Viscount Devlin kept at a distance.'

'We do…or we always have. He approached me in Whiting Street and acted far too friendly for a married man.' Emily arched a dainty eyebrow. 'To escape him I dodged into a building and that's where I bumped into your brother-in-law.' The memory of being pressed against Mark in the dark corridor had spontaneously filled Emily's mind, making her feel rather hot. Briskly she forced herself to concentrate on the mystery of Tarquin's disappearance. 'Mark gave me a ride home and told me you and Jason had spotted Tarquin, but he would not elaborate.'

She understood now why Mark had seemed reticent about identifying Tarquin's companions that evening. It was certainly not considered the done thing for a gentleman to bring to a lady's attention that her brother had been cavorting with loose women, even if the lady in question had just been mistaken for a loose woman herself! She bit at her lip to prevent a wry smile as she wondered what Helen would think on learning she had been mistaken for a harlot.

'Mark must have thought it odd for you to be alone in such an area. Did you tell him you had received a note and had gone there to try to discover Tarquin's whereabouts?'

Emily shook her head. 'I wanted first to find out what the fellow was up to. It would not be the first time Tarquin has created a scandal that we must all try to keep secret.'

'Mark is a trustworthy fellow, you know,' Helen said softly.

Emily put up her chin. There was one thing on which she and Helen tended to be at odds: the worthiness of Mark Hunter. 'He has been horrid to Tarquin in the past.'

'I know you think so…but…oh, let's not debate it now,' Helen said quietly.

Emily's lips twitched in conciliation. 'I would rather you did not tell anyone what we have discussed this morning.'

Helen dipped her head. 'And I will not,' she said huskily. 'Your secrets, as ever, are safe with me. Just as I know mine are with you.'

The two young women exchanged an empathetic smile.

'Brothers!'

'Indeed,' Helen agreed ruefully, for she was no stranger to the selfish behaviour of an older brother. She lifted the teapot, then replaced it. 'I think we need something a little stronger,' she announced and went off to fetch a decanter and two crystal glasses.

Half an hour later, and fortified by a measure of sherry, Emily stepped again into the sunshine in Grosvenor Square. As she walked with the glow of the sun on her head and the sherry a warm coat on her insides, her thoughts again turned to the men troubling her peace of mind. She knew Tarquin ought to dominate her musings, but her memory kept returning to Nicholas Devlin's declaration that he missed her; strangely, she also found herself thinking of the look in Mark Hunter's eyes when they had been pressed close together in the corridor.

With an impatient sigh she increased her pace. The only person who had been likely to shed some light on Tarquin's circumstances was the fellow she'd gone to meet. And how on earth was she to find the rogue now?

She was close to home when she glanced up,

frowning, and through the shimmering atmosphere saw a man coming straight towards her. The fellow was darting furtive looks to the right and left, displaying a crooked nose in profile. Suddenly he darted into an alley between two houses and urgently beckoned to her.

Chapter Six

'**W**ot luck bumping into you, miss.' Mickey's gruff greeting was accompanied by the doffing of his hat. In fact he had been, for some while, loitering about the streets close to Emily's home in the hope of having an opportunity to waylay her.

'What do you have to tell me about my brother?' Emily had briskly recovered from her astonishment at being brought face to face with the ruffian. 'Be assured that you will not collect any winnings from me. I never settle my brother's gambling debts.' She adopted a prim look to impress on him that she was not to be fobbed off with any fantastic yarns designed to make her part with cash. She doubted she would get the whole truth, but was optimistic she might glean a few clues as to what was going on.

Mickey's blue eyes slipped a look left and right and over her shoulder as though to ensure they were private enough. He refused to be rushed into disclosing too much too soon. While he considered tactics he muttered, 'Be more private up there.' He walked away then, with a wag of his head, urging Emily to follow him.

After a moment's hesitation Emily did. It was a narrow gap between the buildings, but an area that was still visible from the main street.

'Ain't about gaming, so don't fret on that. I sent a boy to deliver you a note,' Mickey said as they came to a halt in the alley.

'Yes, I realise it came from you,' Emily retorted sharply. 'I came to Whiting Street and caught sight of you. Why did you leave so suddenly?' She studied his swarthy features. She guessed he was not much older than Tarquin, yet his hair was quite grey and his weatherbeaten skin deeply lined. At close quarters he had an oddly striking, confident appearance. She guessed many people knew him, but she had no idea who he was. 'What is your name and why have you bothered me?'

That enquiry earned her just a crafty squint.

'I put myself to some trouble to meet you in the

City,' Emily pointed out impatiently. 'I hope you are not again wasting my time.'

'I saw Devlin talking to you. I didn't fancy getting tangled with him.'

'You are acquainted with the Viscount?' Emily asked, astonished. She might have thought this fellow of some renown, but had not imagined he might boast an association with a peer of the realm.

Mickey scolded himself for having let that slip. He was canny enough to appreciate that one of his rich and influential clients would not want to acknowledge that he existed.

''Course we ain't acquainted,' Mickey scoffed. 'Just know of him, that's all. And I ain't wasting yer time. Wot I'm about is trying to do you all a favour in case things turn real bad.'

'Has my brother been hurt?' Emily demanded in a whisper. Her mind raced back some years to the time Tarquin had settled a debt at dawn on Wimbledon Common. 'He has duelled before and taken a blade in the shoulder.'

Mickey looked rather startled at knowing that. 'Didn't take him for a fighting fellow.' He shifted his weight. 'Last time I clapped eyes on him he looked right as rain,' he added.

Emily felt a release of tension at knowing it.

''Course if you don't value yer family's reputation, then it's me as is wasting time. I'll be getting off.' Mickey made no move to go and continued slyly peering at Emily from beneath wiry brows.

'Value my family's reputation?' Emily echoed. A ball of lead had settled in her stomach. She had always suspected that eventually something unpleasant would be revealed.

'If you know where Tarquin is you'd be best off telling me,' Mickey urged. 'Then I can warn him 'cos it's sure to leak out if he don't pay up.'

Emily was taken aback as much by the news as by the familiar address he used. Tarquin would surely not class this fellow a friend. 'I do not know where my brother is presently,' Emily said coolly. 'The only reason I came to meet you yesterday was to discover his whereabouts from you.' Disappointment sent a surge of water to her eyes. Angrily Emily dashed it away unwilling to let the rogue see her distress. 'What might leak out? You said this was not about money.'

'Didn't say it weren't about money…said it weren't about gaming.' Mickey Riley's expression had hardened and his voice was little more than a sibilant hiss.

His change in attitude made Emily warily put

distance between them. 'Quickly explain, for I have tarried here with you long enough.'

Mickey shifted sideways to prevent her slipping past him on the path. With a sinister calm he said, 'If you know where he is you'd best let on or I'll have to come knockin' on yer father's door. Poor lass has got nowhere to go, y'see…' Suddenly he interrupted himself with a low curse and shot a frown over Emily's shoulder. With almost comic clumsiness he backed away a yard or two in a few seconds. 'Best finish this another time,' he muttered, then set off briskly up the alley.

Emily spun about to see what had made the fellow abruptly turn tail. She immediately recognised the imposing dark-haired gentleman who was standing by a smart landau. At their ease, and seated in the landau, were her friend, Helen, and her husband, Sir Jason Hunter. The couple were carrying on a laughing conversation with Mark Hunter, who had splayed a hand idly on the glossy coachwork.

Mark was no longer chatting to his brother and sister-in-law, although his smiling expression remained unchanged, and the couple were in no way alerted to the fact that his attention was actually at a distance.

Abruptly Mark gave the landau a final tap and stepped away from it. Emily watched Helen wave at him as the vehicle moved smoothly away heading west.

She had no doubt that Mark had watched her talking to the ruffian, and seen the fellow slope away. She had no doubt too that Mark was about to approach her and ask some awkward questions. He stood sentinel at the mouth of the narrow alley for a moment, trapping her, before strolling very purposefully towards her.

'Miss Beaumont…'

'Mr Hunter…'

The hint of challenge in her tone pulled his mouth wryly aslant.

'Were you again tolerating the company of your troublesome fellow?'

Emily knew immediately to whom he referred, although, of course, Mark was still unaware that Viscount Devlin was the man who had forced her to seek sanctuary in Mr Wilson's office. 'Umm…no… it was not him I was avoiding on Whiting Street.'

'Ah,' Mark said. 'I thought perhaps it might not be him. Of the two of you Riley seemed the more eager to get away just now.'

'Riley?' Emily echoed, testing the name. 'You

know him?' She unconsciously stepped close to Mark to hurry his reply.

'I take it that he did not introduce himself. He must improve his manners.'

Emily coloured faintly at his ironic tone.

'His name is Mickey Riley and I am intrigued to know why you were talking to him.'

While awaiting her answer, and expecting it in any case to be evasive, Mark pondered on the time Mickey Riley and his lady friend had seemed to be watching Emily outside the *modiste*'s shop. He had wondered then if Riley would have the audacity to approach Emily over an unpaid debt of Tarquin's. In his wisdom, he had deduced that Tarquin owed money to Riley over that cockfight. Now his suspicions were straying elsewhere.

He had heard that Mickey Riley procured for a slightly better class of petticoat than the usual drabs who congregated about Covent Garden. Mark, having learned from his brother that Tarquin had last been spotted with a comely harlot in that area, thought it likely that Riley was chasing Tarquin's payment for another vice. In fact, Mark was fearful Mickey Riley was bothering Emily in his role as pimp, not bookie. Tarquin might be ignorant of the fact that his sister was being dragged

into his sordid world, but nevertheless it seemed to
be the case.

'Why were you talking to him?' Mark's voice
was harsh with suppressed anger. Had Tarquin been
within reach he would have throttled him. 'Was
Riley asking you for money?'

Emily immediately bridled at such a curt interrogation. 'I do not see, sir, that our private conversation is any of your business.' She tipped her
blonde head to a confident angle and made to pass
him, but a hand shot to the redbrick wall, blocking
her path.

'Tell me what he wanted.'

Emily curled five fingers over the solid arm beneath his sleeve. The muscle tightened very little in
response to her fierce attempt to move him. Unwilling to participate longer in an undignified tussle, she
snatched back her hand and stepped away from him.
'I repeat, sir, that my conversation with Mr Riley is
none of your business. And your arrogance in de-
manding to know of it is breathtaking.'

'Your naïveté is breathtaking, Miss Beaumont, if
you expect to deal with Riley alone. Besides, you
made all of this my business when you solicited my
help in finding Tarquin. A moment ago you did not
even know Mickey Riley's name. I would hazard a

guess you certainly know nothing about his character or what he does.'

Emily slanted him a mutinous look. Reluctantly she allowed that what he had said was correct. Mark obviously knew that a link existed between Riley and Tarquin and to deny it would be pointless. She had to admit, too, that Tarquin's lengthy absence was becoming a sinister mystery and she felt unequal to solving it alone. She had thus far been allowing her natural antipathy towards Mark to get the better of her. His arrogance needled her, and she certainly did not trust him, but he was rich and powerful and he was Tarquin's friend. She needed just such a gentleman's support for she was sure that Riley would soon return. Without money or physical strength to oil his tongue, she would get nothing from him but more riddles and garbled threats.

She could reveal all to her father, but she was quite sure now that no mild explanation was to be had for her brother's disappearance. When they had been dining with Stephen and his grandmother earlier in the week, her father's melancholy had concerned her. His strained features haunted her mind again now. He was worried for both his sons, not just his firstborn. Emily understood why her parents had encouraged Tarquin to move out of the family home and into his own apartment. They wanted to put distance between Robert and his older brother's excesses in case Robert might follow the example of the brother he idolised.

Conscious she had been some minutes lost in introspection, Emily shot a glance up at Mark. She forged a small smile; it elicited a cynical look.

Mark was not for a moment fooled by her *faux* cordiality and a grimace of impatience impressed on her that he still required an answer to his question.

In a snap she explained, 'Mr Riley sent me a message to meet him in Whiting Street. The note hinted I would get news of Tarquin.' A terse hand flick ridiculed the likelihood. 'It transpires he doesn't know where my brother is. In fact, he expects *me* to disclose to *him* Tarquin's whereabouts.' A glance from beneath her lashes revealed Mark's expression to be unyieldingly stern. 'A moment ago I told Riley I don't know where my brother is, but I'm not sure he believes me.'

'Did you not tell him all that yesterday?'

Emily shook her head. 'I didn't manage to speak to him because…' She hesitated and frowned.

'Because a troublesome fellow scared him off.'

'Yes,' Emily muttered.

'And who was that?' Mark drawled, but his easy tone held an edge of steel.

Emily turned her head, ignoring his probing. 'I have bowed to your bullying and explained about my conversation with Mickey Riley. Please do not annoy me by being too impertinent.'

Emily watched as he leisurely strolled closer. He halted inches away, so close that his broad shoulders completely blocked her view of the road. Slowly he withdrew a hand from where it was lodged in his pocket. Long lean fingers trapped her chin, turned her to look at him.

'I am trying very hard, Miss Beaumont, not to wash my hands of all of this and leave you to your own devices.'

Emily gazed up into eyes of peacock blue and felt her stomach lurch at the threat she read there. Again she bit back defiant words and impressed on herself that this man would have better luck than would she in unearthing Tarquin. His ruggedly handsome face was very close to hers; she blinked as she noticed his long lashes drooping lazily to conceal that he was watching her mouth.

'But you will not abandon me, will you, sir?' The challenge was issued in a voice of silky insolence, and immediately Emily regretted what she had done.

'Will I not?' Mark asked with specious softness. 'And what makes you so sure of that?'

Emily attempted to jerk her face free, but his grip tightened just enough to keep her still.

Very well, if he wanted to know, she would tell him that she knew no noble reason existed for his unexpected helpfulness! But several silent moments later Emily was still finding it difficult to reveal her conceit and accuse him of lusting after her. The more she tried to concentrate on whipping up righteous indignation, and the courage to slander him, the more intensely conscious she was of his touch scorching her jaw.

'Why will I not abandon you?' Mark demanded with veiled amusement. He propped an elbow on the wall and leaned closer. After a moment he felt a surge of tenderness soften his mockery, for her embarrassment was causing her complexion to glow rosily. 'Come, say it. I promise I won't object if you tell me that I'm a fool too susceptible to your beauty and too tolerant of your acid tongue. It's the truth after all.' His fingers extended, caressing a fiery cheek before he abruptly dropped the hand to his side. But he didn't move away and mere inches separated their bodies.

Emily snatched a peek at eyes blackened with desire. *Don't annoy him, you need his assistance*, was the thought racing in her mind. But despite his undeniable usefulness, what really kept her so still and quiet was a longing to again have his cool fingers curving soothingly on her hot cheek. She craved to know how it would feel to have Mark Hunter kiss her.

The yearning was undeniable and, of its own volition, her body seemed to sway forward, her face tilt to tempt a mouth that looked firm and warm...

Mark dipped his head the few inches required to skim together their lips. When she didn't immediately skitter away from that gentle salute, he took immediate advantage. His palms slid to cradle her jaw's sharp fragility and keep her close.

Emily sensed the pressure of his mouth increasing, coaxing her to part her lips while the long fingers, circling softly on her cheeks, continued to skilfully subdue any sensible thought she had of objecting to the liberties he was taking. She yielded to his wooing and her full lips parted to allow his tongue to languidly taste hers. In a daze she rested her weight against him, revelling in the icy fire that was coursing through her limbs. A slow hand travelled to her nape to smooth sensitive places and a delicious shiver passed over Emily, making her sigh against his mouth.

Mark drew her further into his embrace, greatly

aroused by her unexpectedly eager response. His mouth plundered hers sweetly, defying her to protest as his hands slipped beneath her coat to caress her body.

A shock shivered through Emily as his thumbs brushed firmly over her rib cage to stroke the two tender nubs peaking beneath her bodice. Her back was beginning to arch invitingly when suddenly she tensed and her eyes flew wide. A hawker's raucous shout reached her from the street and made her once more alert to where she was…and with whom. She jerked back.

Emily twisted her face free, horribly, shamefully aware that she was behaving like a brazen hussy with a man she knew was firmly attached elsewhere…and in broad daylight too!

She snatched herself from Mark's embrace in two shaky backward steps. Her breathing was ragged as she whispered, 'Thank you, Mr Hunter, for proving to me what I had suspected about you all along.'

Mark's eyes narrowed on her flushed face. Her frigid tone and sparking eyes indicated he was to hear nothing complimentary. 'And what do you suspect about me, my dear?' he gritted out. The first exquisite taste of her had ended too soon and he felt cheated and frustrated.

'I suspect, sir, that you will expect me to reward you for any assistance you give in finding Tarquin.'

'Do you? And what exactly am I expecting to receive?'

Emily blushed scarlet. 'You know very well. And I will not talk indelicately for your titillation.'

Mark tilted his head up and his hands gestured at the sky in exasperation. 'God's teeth! It was just a kiss…and not a very satisfying one at that.'

Emily blanched in mortification. Despite being ashamed of acting the wanton, she couldn't deny she had thought their kiss had been thrilling…but not for him, it seemed.

Mark noticed the fleeting hurt that puckered her features. 'It was nice…sweet…but unfinished,' he explained gently. When she simply tilted her chin and flounced away from him he added, 'You're not yet a woman. When you are you'll understand—'

'Oh, I understand very well,' Emily snapped. She pivoted back to face him to add coolly and quietly, 'I am twenty-four years old and you need not patronise me.'

'I'm not patronising you, I'm appreciating your innocence.'

'Please don't,' Emily countered fiercely. 'Your esteem is not appropriate.'

The silence that followed seemed to echo hollowly between the two high walls on either side of them. Emily jerkily swallowed, immediately regretting that her temper had caused her to unwisely hint at something very private. With her skirts clenched in quivering fists, she attempted to slip past him.

Mark refused to stand aside, although he kept his hands firmly in his pockets. 'My esteem is not appropriate?' he repeated softly. 'Now it has been bestowed I think you owe me an explanation for throwing it back in my face. What is incorrect about my good opinion of your innocence?'

Emily nipped her lower lip in small teeth to prevent an outburst. She had no intention of resuming their previous dialogue. In an icy tone she demanded, 'Please let me pass at once. I have been out too long and my parents will be worried for my safety.'

'I understand their fears; you might have been waylaid by a reprobate.'

'Indeed,' Emily countered with acid amusement. 'But rest assured, I will not mention meeting you.'

Mark gave her a sardonic smile. 'And Riley? Will you tell them about him?'

Emily sent him a stare that might have turned a lesser mortal to stone. Mark unflinchingly returned her regard.

'No. Will you tell them?'

'Not if you'd rather I did not.' He adopted an ironic innocence. 'I swear I require nothing for that favour other than you let me immediately escort you home.'

After a moment of inner turmoil Emily finally capitulated and said sourly, 'Why, thank you, sir, I accept your kind offer.'

Once handed into his curricle, she girded herself for a further interrogation. But he said nothing more at all; the journey passed in silence.

When he politely helped her down in Callison Crescent he said, 'I shall increase my efforts to unearth your brother, but for my benefit as much as yours. There are some pressing matters I would discuss with him.' His vivid eyes veered to her tense face. 'In short, Miss Beaumont, when I drag him back I shall require nothing for the service.'

Emily began her muted thanks, but before their conclusion he was back on the seat and setting off again at speed.

Chapter Seven

'I'll tell you what I told the rest, sir. I haven't seen Mr Beaumont for a good while now. And, if you catch up with the slippery devil, you can tell him from me that I want my rent. If I don't soon get it, I'll set the duns to find him.' With that fervent threat Mrs Dale tried to close the door in Viscount Devlin's face. The toe of one of his polished boots was swiftly wedged on the threshold and prevented her doing so.

'The rest?' Nicholas asked and gave the landlady a smile. 'Other people have been here looking for him?'

Mrs Dale allowed him to push the door a little wider open, her eyes slipping over him in sly assessment. He was Quality, no doubt about it, and might pay her for her time and trouble if she answered a few of his questions. He was probably in a similar situation to hers: owed cash by that wastrel and with no idea how to run him to ground. At the beginning she'd thought Mr Beaumont a fine fellow, with his nice clothes and posh voice, and had no hesitation in renting him rooms.

This house on Westbury Avenue was one of the sounder properties Mrs Dale owned and was in a nice part of town, too. Yet, in her bitter experience, the well-heeled taking suites in Chelsea were no better at paying their rent than were the poor souls cramped in an attic in Whitechapel.

'You said other people have been looking for Mr Beaumont,' Viscount Devlin prompted with ill-concealed irritation at her brooding silence.

The landlady crossed her arms over her shrivelled chest and leaned on the doorjamb. A grimace was aimed at the heavens. 'Mr Beaumont senior came looking for him. Oh, and before that there was a fellow looked like a street bruiser with a bent nose and hair as grey as fog. But a young feller, he seemed, for all that. Then there was a gentleman like yourself… Quality, he were, with fine clothes and a handsome face.' Mrs Dale simpered sideways at the Viscount. 'He had dark hair though, not fair like yours, and might have been taller too.'

'Thank you.' After a cursory nod Nicholas was down the steps and by his carriage.

Having taken up a comfortable position for a lengthy chat, Mrs Dale looked disappointed to see him go so soon. With a cluck of the tongue she turned to go back inside. Realising the nob had left without so much as handing over a farthing she swung back to snarl, 'Tightfist', before slamming the door.

Nicholas got into his carriage, whistling. He had got what he wanted and more besides. Mrs Dale's description of the bruiser was detailed enough for him to be sure that it was Riley who had called looking for Tarquin. He had suspected that Mickey Riley was somehow involved in Tarquin's disappearance. The fellow described as Quality was probably an acquaintance from one of the gaming clubs who was keen to call in his IOU quickly. He was not surprised to learn that Mr Beaumont senior had also been looking for his son. The family would, by now, know he'd absconded. Emily would thus be aware…and concerned…that her brother was in trouble.

She had been in Whiting Street at the same time as had Mickey Riley. Both had seemed oddly alert to the other's presence, yet keen to keep it concealed. Only one reason could account for a meeting between them: Tarquin. Emily must have been summoned by Riley to learn what her brother had been up to. And in return, of course, he would expect a payment.

Nicholas settled back into the squabs with a satisfied smile on his lips. He rapped for his driver to set the coach in motion. One of these nights he ought to make use of the services of that pretty little girl of Mickey's…Jenny, he believed was her name. And while he was there he would have a little talk with Riley and discover if there was a way that Tarquin Beaumont's latest misdemeanour—whatever it was—might benefit them both…

'If you'd rather not attend, I shall convey your regrets.'

It was the pained tone of voice rather than the words spoken that penetrated Emily's deep thoughts. A swift glance at Stephen detected that he was pink with embarrassment. She guessed that he had been talking to her and she had, unwittingly, been ignoring him. 'I'm so sorry, Stephen. What did you say?' Emily blinked beneath her mother's rebuking look.

Before Stephen could answer her Penelope did. 'Stephen was just inviting us to Lady Gerrard's soirée. Isn't that wonderful?' She shot a look at her daughter that dared her to disagree. 'The invitation was issued to Stephen's grandmother, who is her friend, but it has been extended to us too.' Their guest received a grateful smile.

Emily's small teeth sank into her lower lip as she tried to quickly summon up an acceptable excuse. In truth, she lately felt little like socialising. She had a vital and difficult task to undertake and that, together with incessant worries over Tarquin, was dampening her humour.

That morning she had received a note from Nicholas Devlin in which he stressed his pleasure at having finally had a chance to talk privately to her. The note had ended with him expressing a *great desire* that they might soon find another such opportunity. Emily had been stunned to receive it, and her first instinct had been to throw it on the fire. She might once have loved him, and been on the point of becoming his wife, but it had all turned to ashes years ago. He had married another woman and Frances was increasing with his child.

The Viscount's letter to her, like his attitude on Whiting Street, was highly irregular to say the least. Emily had a suspicion that it was not a simple friendship that Nicholas was angling for, but a more intimate relationship. But it was finished between them. She was a mature woman now, not a silly girl just out of the schoolroom. She was able to control her senses and her future, and she had no intention of allowing a married man to so much as kiss her.

If she simply ignored his letter, he might be encouraged to send another. She had to let him know immediately, and in strong terms, that pursuing her was a lost cause—he would never again seduce her into wantonness.

Hard on the heels of her virtuous resolve came a very disturbing truth: *Another gentleman had very recently and very easily made her act the wanton and the incident was impossible to put from her mind.*

Emily fidgeted on her seat as phantom pressure from warm hard lips teased her mouth. She spitefully sank her teeth into the tingling skin to stop the sensation.

Tarquin… Viscount Devlin… She could accept that those gentlemen would be bothering her peace of mind, for both had given her due cause. But the most persistent images in her head were of Mark Hunter and what had occurred between them in the alleyway. And she wanted to dismiss that as inconsequential…as he had.

It was simply pique, she told herself. No woman

would like to have a kiss—whether it had been welcome or not—dismissed by a gentleman with such a lack of gallantry. Neither could she be pleased with herself for having hinted she was unchaste. Would he have already forgotten what she said? Or was he mulling it over and deeming her quite capable of being a sullied woman?

This time it was a long and sibilant sigh from her mother that startled her to the present.

'My…you are in a daydream today, Emily.' Penelope chirped a brittle laugh. 'Perhaps another cup of tea might liven you a little and help you concentrate.'

Emily murmured an apology. Indeed, she felt guilty for having again failed to talk to Stephen. He was a fine gentleman and deserved better than being ignored while her mind was preoccupied with the less worthy. 'You must thank your grandmother, Stephen, for thinking of us and securing such an invitation—'

'Well, that's settled then,' Penelope Beaumont interjected swiftly, before Emily could conclude her declination.

'The invitation is also extended to your friend Sarah Harper.' Stephen's muted pleasure at her acceptance spoke volumes. Emily realised he was well aware that she would rather not attend. 'Grandmama mentioned to Fiona Gerrard that you might like a young lady of your own age to accompany you. Not that there won't be other young ladies present, of course. But you might not know any of them well enough to chat to…' he finished lamely.

'If you are to be there, Stephen, I shall have a friend to talk to,' Emily said and gave him a comforting smile. She could not now cry off without causing a fuss and thus graciously accepted her defeat. 'But I'm certain Sarah would be pleased to go too. I shall call on her later and find out for sure.'

When Stephen had gone Penelope surged to her feet and clapped her hands in delight. 'Only think…Fiona Gerrard's soirée! Augusta might be a rum old bird, but she has very influential friends, it seems. I expect she has secured us such a prized invitation to make up for being impolite when she came here to dine.'

'Perhaps.' Emily gave a slight smile. 'A mere few days ago you were hoping Augusta would be on her way back to Bath by now.'

'I know…and I don't mind admitting that I hoped the old harridan might make the journey in a hearse.' Penelope smiled wickedly. 'Now I'm hoping dear Augusta might stay in London all Season. Who knows how many times we might be guests of Lady Gerrard? It might be a very happy time for you.'

Emily slipped her mother a shrewd look from silver eyes. 'In what way are you hoping I might benefit, Mama?'

'I think you know quite well, young lady.' But Penelope went on to explain, 'Lady Gerrard is known to have a host of eligible bachelors in her circle. We must make sure you look your very best—you might catch the eye of one of them.'

'And what of Stephen?' Emily asked wryly. 'Is he now to be discouraged?'

'Not at all!' Penelope gasped. 'We need a nice gentleman in reserve. By Michaelmas you *must* be spoken for. You cannot sit another year on the shelf. Oh…here's your father home at last.' Penelope rushed into the hallway to recount to him her exciting news.

Having listened with furrowed brow to his wife, Mr Beaumont nodded absently and made to walk on towards his study.

Penelope looked affronted by his lack of enthusiasm. 'Well! I really think you could show a little more interest in such a promising opportunity for your only daughter. Your only daughter who, I might add, is worryingly close to her twenty-fifth birthday!'

Cecil turned about and gave an apologetic sigh. 'I'm sorry, my dear, but lately I am too concerned over Tarquin's whereabouts to take heed of much at all. I have been to several of his haunts and all the clubs in St. James's. Nobody has any news of him. It has been a confounded long while since I had word from my heir.'

Emily had ventured into the hallway and heard what her grim-faced father said about his errant son. Strain was etched deeply about his weary eyes and Emily felt herself seething with anger at Tarquin.

For a moment she was tempted to blurt out to her father that she knew more than he did. But what comfort would there be for him in knowing that the ruffian who had been loitering about was issuing threats in his quest to locate Tarquin? Neither would her parents relish knowing that the last news of their eldest son was of him cavorting with harlots in Covent Garden. Indeed, should she disclose what she knew, it was sure to increase her father's anxiety, and make her mother quite hysterical.

'He will turn up soon enough, Papa. I know Mark Hunter is searching for him, too.' Emily said encouragingly.

'Our son is the most selfish wretch imaginable!' Penelope suddenly burst out. 'All the while we must concentrate on him…only him! Well, I refuse to let his shenanigans spoil our outing to Lady Gerrard's.

We will go, and we will enjoy ourselves!' Penelope shot a look between her husband and her daughter. 'I forbid another mention of Tarquin until the weekend!'

The sleek carriage slowed to a stop. After waiting and watching for a few minutes Viscount Devlin spotted, at a distance, the fellow he had been hoping would appear. He alighted and pulled his many-caped coat protectively about his elegant shoulders. With sheer distaste puckering his features, he began to pick a path, with the help of his cane, over dirt and debris underfoot. As he walked the gloomy lane, shadowy female bodies brushed against him, murmuring lewdly. He ignored them and roughly pushed away one bold harlot who persisted in clinging to his arm.

Crossing the road he approached a gin house spewing a pool of lamplight on to slimy cobbles. As he came closer, its raucous sound deadened the monotonous hum of begging irritating his brain.

'Riley.'

His quarry spun about on hearing his name, and stared warily at Devlin as he stepped purposefully closer. 'Evenin' to you, sir.' His tongue snaked over his lips. 'Here for business?'

'Why else?' Nicholas sneered sarcastically and gave a speaking look at his squalid surroundings.

Mickey grimaced understanding, but his eyes were narrowed and alert. He hadn't forgotten that this man had seen him in Whiting Street when he was there to meet Beaumont's sister. And he was suspicious that the fine fellow was here for information, not pleasure.

'Got a new girl called Lucy might take yer fancy. Young and fresh she is,' Mickey said, hoping to distract any awkward questions by arousing the fellow's lust.

'I'll take Jenny.'

Mickey shot a look at him. 'She's laid up…no use tonight…'

'In that case, perhaps there's another bit of business we might do.' Two drunken navvies swayed past, arm in arm, roaring with laughter. Nicholas waited for them to weave away before gritting, 'Is there a better place we might go to discuss this?'

Mickey chewed the inside of his cheek. Any mention of business pricked up his ears, but he didn't trust this man. He didn't trust him one bit. In fact, he'd sooner deal with Old Nick himself.

Noting his hesitation, Nicholas purred coaxingly, 'There will be a tidy bit of blunt in this for you if things work out the way I like.'

It was what Mickey needed to hear. With a flick

of his beady eyes to right and to left, he cocked his head and led the Viscount through an iron gateway. The alleyway led to a small door and Mickey indicated the Viscount should enter.

Inside, revellers could be heard through the wall, showing they were immediately behind the gin shop. The room held the unmistakable reek of poverty, and a few battered pieces of furniture.

Noting the Viscount's disgust, Mickey said sardonically, 'Best I can do at short notice. So if it ain't a woman you're after tonight, what can I do fer yer?'

'You can tell me why you were on Whiting Street to meet Tarquin Beaumont's sister.'

Mickey's tongue tip hovered over his lips. 'Who?' he piped, all innocence.

Devlin smiled thinly. 'Don't act the fool and don't bother lying. I know you were on Whiting Street to meet her.'

'Told you that, did she?'

Devlin paced about the room, trying to find a spot where the atmosphere was less fetid. He came close to Mickey and looked directly into his eyes, for they were of similar height. 'I know Miss Beaumont is trying to find her brother, and I would like to assist. That would please her. She might in turn then please me.'

Mickey gave a sly smile. 'Ah…so you'd like to please Miss Beaumont…and have her please you…'

'Indeed I would,' Nicholas drawled

'And you think I might be able to help.'

'Yes.'

Mickey gave a chuckle. 'That's a thought, sir. That's certainly a thought, and it is wot I do best. But it's a bit risky with a classy lady 'cos there's her family to consider.'

Viscount Devlin reached into an inside pocket and withdrew a silk purse. It was bulging fit to burst the seams. He leisurely slackened the drawstring and drew forth a gold sovereign. The glinting disc was held between thumb and forefinger while he shook the sack until chinking could be heard. His top lip curled as he saw Mickey's eyes pounce greedily on the cash. 'There's twice that amount for you if it all goes to plan.'

Mickey shot a look at Devlin. He grinned, but his eyes were crafty slits. 'You've come to the right place, sir. I'm sure that if Miss Beaumont got news that her brother were laid up somewhere, say somewhere quiet and very private, and him right poorly, well, I reckon she'd go there straight off to see him.'

'I think so too,' Nicholas Devlin said dulcetly. 'I'm glad we understand one another.'

Mickey nodded.

'Did you tell Miss Beaumont where her brother is hiding?'

Mickey shook his head, snorting a laugh. 'I don't know where the wily cove is, but she knows well enough that I'm on his tail, for I told her so straight.'

At Viscount Devlin's enquiring look, Mickey brusquely explained, 'I got a bit of business of me own to sort out with Beaumont. Nuthin' that needs put a dampener on wot we just discussed.'

'Good,' Nicholas said. 'You understand that we have not had a conversation of any sort?'

Mickey gave a bark of surly laughter. 'Respectable gent like you…talk to the likes of me? Who'd believe that?'

Nicholas gave a nod.

'I'll see what I can do. Where can I contact you?' Mickey asked.

'You can't. And don't ever try to. I'll return in a few days or so.' Devlin turned towards the door, his nostrils flaring at the stench. 'Let me out of this fleapit.'

Mickey sprang to open the door.

'This new girl…she's young and fresh, you say?'

'She is indeed. Shall I fetch her?' Mickey started to close the door again.

'Not here, you fool,' the Viscount barked with utter contempt. 'My carriage is close by in Houndsditch. Send her there.'

Chapter Eight

Mark Hunter stepped swiftly into shadows to watch the black-cloaked figure traversing the rough cobbles. On reaching his carriage the Viscount sprang in, unaware he had been observed, and closed the door.

That Nick Devlin was sordid enough to seek pleasure in such a stew did not surprise Mark. Indeed, he had spotted him on other occasions doing business with whores in London's back streets. But an idea stirred in his mind that another reason might have brought Devlin here tonight. Had the Viscount forgone the comfort of Mayfair to come, as he had, in search of Riley and some answers?

The only connection between Tarquin and Devlin that Mark knew of was a mutual loathing. After a moment he grunted a soft, self-mocking laugh. He was being too fanciful. Why would Devlin give a damn about Tarquin's whereabouts? It was far more likely to be lust, not hatred, that had urged Nick to visit this haunt.

Pushing away from the wall, Mark was about to approach the gin shop when he heard soft footfalls and drew back against the brick once more. A young woman emerged from the murk and came towards him. Fleetingly their eyes met as she gazed, wide-eyed, up at him. But she didn't speak or accost him. She hurried on past, winding tighter about her head a shawl covering a thatch of curly fair hair.

Mark pivoted on a heel to watch her. He had been surprised by her looks. She wasn't raddled or dead-eyed as were many jades. But then the girl looked only about fifteen and had not yet lost the optimism of youth. She halted by Devlin's carriage and used her fist to bang on the door. Within a moment she had unceremoniously hiked up her skirts and disappeared inside. The vehicle remained stationary, although within seconds the carriage lamp began to swing on its hook.

Mark's mouth thinned in disgust as he realised that Devlin could not even be bothered to take her somewhere more discreet. But of course he had no idea he had been noticed by one of his peers, being serviced by a whore in Houndsditch. The locals sloping around might know the Viscount by sight, and know what he was about, but that would not worry Devlin. However, talk of his debauchery, in polite society salons, might.

Mark had never liked Nick Devlin. Even before he had married the sister of one of his friends, simply for her fortune, he had despised the man for his deviousness.

Mark was aware that Emily had been engaged to Devlin about four years ago. He and Tarquin had then been barely acquainted and he had not known Emily at all at that time. Before this precise moment Mark had never given much thought to what had broken the betrothal between Miss Beaumont and the Viscount, or what had ignited the burning enmity between Tarquin and Devlin. But now he viewed things differently. Lately Emily Beaumont had been arousing his curiosity…as well as his body. He wanted to know about her life, past and present, and why she would once have agreed to marry such a character as Nicholas Devlin.

Mickey Riley spat out an oath beneath his breath. Was he never to be left to his own devices this evening? Again he slipped a look from beneath lowered lashes while trying to guess what this individual wanted. He certainly wasn't a customer, but then there was always a first time for a bit of rough trade, even for fellows who seemed like they had never stepped foot outside Mayfair, and could afford a top-notch bit of muslin.

Mickey felt uneasy, for he twice had seen this gent talking to Miss Beaumont and it seemed an odd coincidence that he should turn up just after the Viscount had been by with a wicked suggestion concerning that very lady.

The fellow was getting closer and Mickey cursed again that he had ever got involved with Tarquin Beaumont. He was beginning to think Jenny was right: they should have forgotten all about him and moved on to someone with deeper pockets. Beaumont was of good stock and looked flush, but nevertheless Mickey was coming to fear the wastrel might not have two ha'pennies of his own to rub together.

The Viscount was a better class of nob; he'd seen the proof of his quality bulging in that silk bag. And there was a way he could get his hands on the cash. If Tarquin turned out to be a dud, he'd have to make sure that his sister made up for the loss…

But now this damnable fellow was prowling

about. Mickey felt his hackles stir and belatedly
tried to slip out of sight through the gate. If he'd discovered what the Viscount was about he'd be here
to do battle for the lady's honour.

As Mark watched the pimp scuttling away, he
felt a side of his mouth tug into a smile. So Riley
had guessed what he wanted and it didn't look as
though he was willing to provide any answers to his
questions. Mark quickened his pace, following Riley
through the gate and into the alley.

'You need us, Mickey?'

The bellowed offer of assistance came from the
street where a couple of strapping young men stood
belligerently eyeing the casual interloper.

Mickey slid a nervous glance up at his stalker. In
an odd way he found him more intimidating than
Devlin. He was taller and broader, but he sensed in
him a power that was not just about physical
strength. 'Do I need 'em? Or are you here tonight
just fer business, sir?'

'I'm here for information. I'm willing to pay for
your time.' Mark gave a slight smile. 'So…business
it is…'

Mickey's eyes narrowed in admiration. He was
a courageous nob, he'd give him that. He didn't
seem at all put out on knowing that, with a click of

his fingers, Mickey could set a couple of his hounds on him.

'I only got to shout and they'll be back.' Mickey flicked a hand, dismissing his associates. The fellow didn't look as though he'd come for a brawl. His manner was straightforward and his rig-out expensive. Besides, the promise of payment always mellowed Mickey's misgivings. He turned and opened the door, mockingly inviting his elegant visitor to enter.

As his eyes flitted over squalor, lit by a solitary oil lamp, a faint frown was all that betrayed Mark's distaste. He launched straight away into, 'I should introduce myself. I'm Mark Hunter and Tarquin Beaumont is a good friend of mine. Why have you been bothering Mr Beaumont's sister, and asking after her brother's whereabouts?'

Mickey cocked his head to an insolent angle. 'Not been bothering her, been trying to help,' he contradicted.

'In what way?'

Mickey turned a sly eye up to a hard, shadowy visage. 'Well, now…that's private and confidential…just between me and the Beaumonts.'

Mark reached into his coat and withdrew a bank note. 'They don't want to be bothered with it all.' He waved the money held in thumb and forefinger. 'I said I'd pay for your time and information.'

Mickey reflexively stuck out a hand, his eyes fixed on the plentiful cash.

Mark lazily crushed the paper in a broad palm. 'First answer me—and give me the truth, or you'll get nothing.'

'Beaumont's acted foolish, and I reckon if I can find him, and make him pay what's necessary, it'll save the family being made a laughing-stock. That's all I wanted to see Miss Beaumont about. You can ask her.'

'I don't need to. She has already told me what you spoke about. You haven't told me anything I, or any one else, doesn't already know about Tarquin Beaumont. The family's reputation will survive another tale of him losing his shirt at the tables.'

'Ain't gaming.' Mickey's voice was sulky.

'What, then?' Mark purred. 'Has he been keeping company with your whores, and not paying you fast enough for their services?'

Mickey gave a lopsided smile. 'Well, now, Mr Hunter, you're getting closer, but I can tell you, you still ain't quite right.'

'And I can tell you, I'm getting tired of playing games.' The hand holding the cash was thrust impatiently into Mark's pocket. 'Have you set your bully boys on him and he's fled?'

Mickey crossed his arms over his chest. 'Ain't done that at all,' he said airily. 'But he has taken off and all 'cos of a woman.'

'Go on.'

'Not until you pay, and I want that and another the same.' He nodded his head at the pocket hiding the banknote. Mickey's ferreting brain had realised that there was indeed a way to make money from the Beaumonts. He could recoup his losses twice over. Devlin would pay for fun with the sister, and Hunter would pay for information about the brother's folly.

Mark gave him the cash with a perilous glower that made Mickey quickly blurt out, 'Her name's Jenny and he took a real shine to her right from the start…'

Fifteen minutes later Mark was striding back along the slimy cobbles with an expression as dark and forbidding as his environment. *Tarquin, you bloody fool!* was the thought rotating in his mind as he vaulted into his carriage and gave directions for it to head home.

'You look like an angel.'

Emily gave her ardent-eyed admirer a smile and

absently smoothed her fingers over the ivory silk of her skirt. It had been her mother's idea that she wear the pale, dainty dress; Emily had favoured wearing blue satin, which she thought suited her colouring and looked less…virginal. But she had not felt inclined to argue over something trivial when so much that was serious was occupying her mind.

Despite still having had no news of Tarquin, she considered her mother to be right in one respect: they rarely were invited to be entertained at such a fine address.

Before leaving the house this evening she had dashed off a concise note to Nicholas and, when handing it to Millie to take to the post, had felt pleased that she had allowed it to take up so little of her time. Emily felt lighter in spirits than she had in a while. She looked about at her scintillating surroundings. They ought to enjoy the outing and forget their woes for a few hours.

Stephen politely held out an arm to her, then one to her friend Sarah. 'We must find some chairs in the music room before the orchestra starts. There is sure to be a crush later.'

As they walked, Sarah whispered, awestruck, 'I'm so glad you asked me to come with you. This is quite the most impressive place I have ever entered.'

Emily gave a slow nod as her eyes flitted over the opulent appointments of Lady Gerrard's drawing room. 'Indeed it is wonderful.'

'Her late husband died five years ago and left Fiona very rich indeed,' Stephen contributed to the conversation. 'But she has a host of influential friends to ease her pain at his passing.' He nodded to Sir Jason Hunter, who was just entering the room with his wife. 'Here is one of the most distinguished, just arrived.'

'Oh, Helen is here,' Emily said, with a pleased smile, on seeing her friend. 'Let's go and say hello.'

Barely a moment after they had joined Sir Jason and Lady Hunter, Emily's eyes were drawn away from the handsome couple and to the doorway. Framed in the aperture and, she had to admit, looking quite magnificent in a slate-grey tailcoat and buff trousers, was a tall dark-haired gentleman she immediately recognised. But what caused her to quickly blink and look away was not the fact that the paragon's eyes were steadily on her, but that his presence had caused her stomach to somersault.

Noting Emily's slight flush, Helen casually turned her head. 'Your brother has arrived,' she told her husband while giving Emily an astute look.

As Emily was murmuring about moving on to the music room with her friends, Mark joined their group.

'We were just off to listen to the concert,' Jason told his brother, his hand welcoming his wife's delicate fingers on his sleeve.

Sarah suddenly took Stephen's elbow and, ignoring his rather startled expression and reluctance to go, steered him to follow Sir Jason and his wife.

When the couples had moved away a few paces, Mark looked down at the top of a shiny crown of blonde hair. 'Am I forgiven yet?' he asked huskily.

'I'm afraid not, Mr Hunter,' Emily said stiffly. Her elbow-length lace gloves were smoothed over shapely arms and she made a move to follow her friends.

'Perhaps if I tell you that I have come here just to see you, and have some news of Tarquin, you might think more kindly of me.'

Emily immediately pivoted back to face him. She tilted her chin to a confident angle, but her hands were tightly clasped to still their quivering. 'Is that true, or just a ruse to make me stay a while longer with you?'

'Why are you afraid of staying a while longer with me, Emily?' Mark asked softly. 'Do you imagine I might try to kiss you in Lady Gerrard's drawing room?'

Emily blushed to the roots of her golden hair, but

managed to say, 'Not at all. I'm sure in company you adopt the manner of a perfect gentleman.' Her silver eyes flashed at him. 'Besides, why would you bother when you're sure to again be disappointed?'

Mark's soft laugh was directed over the top of Emily's head. 'Ah…so that still rankles, does it?' he murmured. 'I explained at the time why I said it, and paid you a compliment in the process. Which reminds me that you still owe me an explanation for finding fault with my praise.'

Emily felt her heart jump to her throat. She knew exactly to what he referred, and had no intention of resuming *that* conversation. She quickly changed subject. 'I had no idea you would be here tonight.' A hint of blame sharpened her tone.

'I gather you would rather I was not.'

'You overestimate the matter, sir,' Emily returned coolly. 'You may stay or go and it will make no difference whatsoever to me.'

Mark's eyes held hers until Emily flushed and looked away. 'Is that so?' he softly drawled. 'Well, as I came solely to see you, I think I shall go.' With a slight nod of his dark head he turned and was soon strolling towards the door.

In mortification Emily watched his broad back. He was actually going to leave, and she had not yet discovered what news he had of Tarquin. She bit down on her lower lip to control herself, for she was tempted to call him back. She had been so disturbed by those silly emotions that came to the fore when in close proximity to the dratted man that she had not quizzed him over her brother. And now she might have lost the chance.

She was obliquely aware that more people were moving away towards the music room. Strains of a melody reached her ears, but her eyes were focused on an athletic figure that would be soon lost from sight.

With an indrawn breath, and her pearly teeth clenched together, she went in pursuit of him, weaving nimbly through guests who were, in the main, proceeding in the opposite direction.

'Mr Hunter!' She was sure he had heard her call his name, but was ignoring her. With tears of frustration spiking her eyes, Emily yanked on one of his elbows, then quickly stumbled back a few paces as he turned about.

'I can't believe you would actually go before telling me what you have discovered about Tarquin,' she gritted out in an undertone. 'Your pride is too easily wounded, sir.'

'Is that an apology?'

She had expected Mark might look smug at having humbled her into chasing him, but his expression was remarkably grave.

'If you require I give one…yes…it is.' Emily tilted her chin and squarely met his vivid blue eyes.

A corner of Mark's mouth tilted and an idle glance swept the sparsely populated room. 'I don't require anything from you not freely given, Emily.'

Emily felt herself heating beneath his steady regard. So he couldn't resist reminding her that she had willingly participated in that kiss.

'You look a little flushed. Let me accompany you to the terrace for a breath of fresh air.' A nod of Mark's head indicated doors that were adjacent to them.

Emily looked to the right and to the left. The room was almost deserted. 'It is private enough here for you to tell me what you have discovered.'

'I think the terrace might be a better place. What I have to report is quite bad news and it is amazing how walls can sprout ears.' As though to prove him wise a young lady obligingly emerged from behind a marble pillar where she had been adjusting a bow on her bodice. She sent them a sly look before gliding away towards the music room.

'You have nothing to fear from me, Emily.' Mark's voice was husky with sincerity, although a vaguely mocking light was in his eyes. 'I shall do nothing to displease you.'

Emily snapped her eyes from his. He knew very well that another kiss from him was likely to have the reverse effect! Just as her defences were beginning to crumble she had a glimpse of someone who made her determinedly put back the barriers.

Mark's mistress was just taking a seat in the music room, near to the doors. Barbara didn't appear to have noticed that her lover was conversing privately with another woman. Or perhaps she had seen them talking together, but didn't care. The sophisticated brunette was undoubtedly confident enough of her position in Mark's life to ignore silly women like her who secretly found Mark Hunter fascinating.

If Mark had noticed his mistress he gave no sign. His attention remained steadily on Emily while he patiently awaited permission to escort her to the terrace.

Emily felt her temper rising. He had the nerve to say he had come simply to see her, when in fact he was here with his mistress! He had the gall to remind her of stolen kisses…to flirt with her and want to take her into the dark…despite being partnered this evening by the woman he loved!

Mark had sensed the atmosphere between them had been on the point of thawing. Now it seemed frostier than ever. He took a glance about to see what had changed Emily's humour and glimpsed Barbara staring at them. A footman closed the doors to the music room, cutting off her view of them, as Mark's lips formed a soundless oath. He had not imagined that his mistress would attend this soirée. Barbara and Lady Gerrard were not the best of friends, and he had felt confident that he would spend an evening free of Barbara's constant surveillance. For some months her possessiveness, and unsubtle hints about marriage, had been irritating him.

'It is probably best we do not talk now,' Emily said glacially. 'Might I suggest we meet tomorrow? I shall ensure that I am by the water in Hyde Park at about four in the afternoon. You may then tell me what you know.' Without awaiting a reply she turned to move away.

'If you're expecting me to be at your beck and call, you will be disappointed. I won't be there.'

Emily swirled about and glared at him in frustration. 'In that case, tell me quickly now about my brother.'

'Come to the terrace, and I shall.'

Emily stepped angrily towards him. 'I think you know, sir, that I ought not do that. And I am amazed that you would suggest such a thing when our friends and family are close by to witness it. You might not have a reputation to keep, but I have!' Emily felt her face becoming pink beneath his lazy low-lidded regard. In that instant she was sure they both had in mind her implication that her innocence was lost. Recklessly she added, 'And Mrs Emerson is sure to soon wonder where you are.'

'I didn't know that Mrs Emerson would be here tonight.'

A huff of contemptuous laughter made a pout of Emily's soft lips. She might have appeared insouciant, but inwardly she squirmed with embarrassment for behaving in such an unseemly manner. Young ladies did not hint they knew of a gentleman's *amours*, least of all to the gentleman himself.

'I was about to go home a moment ago. You might not consider me mannerly, Emily, but I assure you, had I escorted Mrs Emerson here, I would have been polite enough to inform her I was leaving.' With that cutting remark he executed a crisp bow and walked away. When he reached the door he hesitated, then looked back to see that Emily was standing quite still where he had left her.

As though in a trance she took a small step, then another and another, until she was walking quite quickly towards the French doors.

Chapter Nine

A scent of early blossom teased Emily's nostrils as she stepped on to the granite flags. Her eyes strained to identify shapes in shadows, for merely a sliver of silver illuminated the ebony heavens. After a moment she could see that the terrace was enclosed by stone balustrade; to one side was a little bench snugly set in an ivy-tangled trellis. A gusting breeze brought a tinkle of water to her ears, but she couldn't locate the fountain. Emily gazed up wistfully at a few winking stars. It was an undeniably romantic setting and, had the attractive gentleman escorting her been someone she liked and trusted, she might have been tempted to let him steal a kiss…or two…

Emily swiftly put such wild imaginings from her mind and paid attention to the undeniably handsome features of her companion. 'Have you discovered Tarquin's whereabouts, Mr Hunter?' she asked briskly.

'Finding him is not the problem. I could unearth him quite quickly if I wanted to.' Mark strolled to the stone rail and, bracing a hand against it, contemplated the gardens.

'Why on earth haven't you done so?' Emily demanded on a gasp.

'I haven't done so because at the moment it might be prudent to leave him out of sight. A scandal might break on his return home.'

Emily felt blood seep from her complexion to leave it tingling icily. His tone had been harsh, indicating that a very bleak announcement was yet to come. 'He is in bad trouble, isn't he?' she murmured.

'I suppose it could be worse. As far as I know, he isn't dead or injured…'

His sarcasm simply strengthened Emily's anxiety and she made a frantic guess at what ordeal they might yet face. 'Has he duelled again and killed a man this time? Are his family out for Tarquin's blood?'

'It's nothing of the sort, Emily,' Mark reassured, his stern profile softening. 'Your brother has undoubtedly been foolish, but not criminal.'

Emily nodded quickly, gratefully, indicating she was ready to hear the worst of it.

Mark stuffed his hands into his pockets and turned to face her. He cast down his eyes, his expression contemplative, as he sought an appropriate way of relating a sordid tale. A good deal of young men, while drunk, had been unruly and lived to regret it. Mark was no exception to that rule. But generally a gentleman strove to be discreet, and protect himself and his family from the consequences of his excesses. He certainly avoided binding himself to his sinful past. 'I told you that Tarquin hasn't been seen since my brother spotted him loitering in Covent Garden,' he carefully began to explain.

'Yes,' Emily breathed. 'And I know he was consorting with harlots that night.' She swallowed her embarrassment at the indelicate turn to their conversation. 'I understand why you said nothing; it is an awkward subject for a gentleman to discuss with a lady.' She delicately coughed. 'But I think we both know protocol is of scant importance at present.'

'Who told you about that?' Mark frowned, for his memory had immediately pounced on the fact that Nick Devlin had recently been in Riley's company. The Viscount was an unpleasant character and he certainly hated Tarquin. But surely even he would not be so mean as to bring to a sister's attention her brother's lechery?

'Helen told me she had seen Tarquin on that occasion in Covent Garden. We are intimate friends, and able to talk about anything at all…good or bad…' Emily said by way of explanation.

'As you know that much, you should also know that Mickey Riley is a pimp. I tracked down Riley in Houndsditch and he told me why Tarquin has gone into hiding.' Mark swiped a hand across his jaw as he looked down into a visage of pure pale beauty. Emily's luminous eyes were hungrily fixed on his face, but it was just information she wanted from him, whereas what he wanted… One of his hands started to travel towards her, but before he could sense the warm skin of her complexion beneath his fingers they were brought back to the cold stone ledge.

He felt selfish for wanting to touch. He wanted to offer comfort, but it was primarily desire that had urged him to reach for her. He took a few steps away, removing himself from temptation. 'Your brother took a shine to one of Riley's women,' Mark informed huskily. 'Her name is Jenny and Tarquin had visited her on several occasions. The last time they met he was allegedly very drunk and very amorous.'

Emily swallowed the hard lump forming in her

throat. She could tell that Mark was uneasy about giving full details of the disaster. Obviously it was of a vulgar nature. Suddenly she guessed what it might be. Once the awful thought was in her mind she had to know. 'Are you about to tell me that my brother has fathered a bastard?'

Mark frowned pensively. 'Mickey Riley didn't make mention of a child. But if there is one, now or in the future, it won't be a bastard. Your brother has married Jenny.'

'*Married?* Tarquin has married a *harlot*?' Emily's voice was little above a whisper and her eyes were enormous dark pools in a face that might have been carved in white marble. Suddenly she gasped a laugh. 'The rogue is lying! Riley probably hopes to extort money from us with a ridiculous trumped-up tale. Tarquin is a gamester, not a womaniser. I'm sure he has never given marriage, even to a respectable lady, a single thought.'

'I've no doubt Jenny was exceptionally persuasive,' Mark said in a tone of dark irony. 'And Riley isn't lying.' His expression became sober. 'I made him divulge the whereabouts of the minister alleged to have performed the ceremony. Today I visited Jeremiah Plumb. He is not a very savoury character, but he is a man of the cloth and remembers the couple. It seems the marriage is valid.'

Emily blinked to clear the mist from her eyes. Agitatedly she twisted this way and that before coming to a halt facing the darkling gardens. Her hands gripped tightly at the balustrade and her blonde head dipped in despair towards them.

Mark positioned himself just behind her slender form, resting his palms comfortingly on shoulders that were tense and shaking. When she did not immediately shrug him off, his thumbs stroked with tender sensuality against her flesh. 'I'm sorry to be the one to bring such bad tidings. But you did want to know.'

Emily nodded morosely. 'The selfish…stupid… wretch!' she suddenly spat though small pearly teeth. She spun about and gazed up at him with tear-glossed eyes. 'He has given no thought again to how this will hurt our parents. Or how it might affect Robert. Robert idolises him, yet he has shown him no proper example, as an older brother should. If Robert were to be led astray by such behaviour, it would break our parents' hearts.' Her muted outrage ended on a watery choke. The lulling sensation of Mark's fingers moving on her skin calmed her, and she stayed within his casual embrace, her mind furiously working. 'Now I understand what Riley is about. He is urgently seeking Tarquin so he can blackmail him. He wants money for his silence. But even if we pay what he asks, what good will it do? Sooner or later it will all come out.' Her voice trembled into depressive quiet.

Mark slowly slid a hand to her nape, soothing softly beneath silky blonde curls. His dark head bent close to her, his lips discreetly skimming a crown of scented hair. 'Hush… Riley can be dealt with quite easily. And a divorce can be arranged. It will be possible to contain the worst of the scandal, I'm sure.'

'Do you truly think so?' Emily clung to his sleeves, shook them a little to drag from him more reassurance.

'I do,' Mark stressed gently and urged her closer to him. He lowered his head and touched his lips lightly to hers. It was a mild salute, almost passionless.

The anguish churning Emily's stomach was slowly transforming into an infinitely nicer sensation. Warmth was stealing through her cool limbs, bringing a welcome relaxation to her tight muscles. What she had just learned had obliterated all memory of Mark's mistress, of her vow to shun his advances, from her mind. She simply yearned for more sweet relief from fretting on an impending calamity. She closed her eyes in wordless agreement.

Mark was swift to oblige. His mouth slid against hers with more pressure this time, tenderly persuading her soft lips to part, allowing him to taste the warm silk within.

Emily pressed closer, needing his strength and protection. When his firm hands started to trace her silhouette, she clung to him, responding to his artful caresses with sighing pleasure. A sudden noise shattered the spell.

Mark cursed beneath his breath as he noticed that the terrace doors were being brushed back and forth by a low branch of a tree. 'There's nobody there; it's just the wind strengthening,' he murmured as Emily would have pulled away.

She relaxed again, accepting the comfort of the strong arms that bound her to him. Quite naturally her face found a nook beneath his shoulder in which to nestle. But even as she craved again to feel his mouth on hers, her mind was clogged with questions. 'But…what if…what if there *is* a child?' she insisted with a hint of hysteria. 'What on earth is to be done then?'

With a quivering hand silencing her gasp of dismay, Barbara Emerson retreated from where she had been eavesdropping by the French doors. From the moment she had seen Mark talking to Emily Beaumont in the drawing room, her instinct had been to find out what was going on. Since the afternoon when they had all met by chance outside the *modiste*'s, she had been alert to Mark's attraction to Emily.

After her husband had died Barbara had taken great pains to lure Mark back to her. She had been sure that she could kindle his continuing desire for her into love. Then she would get him to marry her once a decent period of mourning was done.

But years had passed since then and, although Barbara was sure she was the most important woman in Mark's life, she had accepted she would never again be the only one. She knew of his brief liaisons with a society beauty here or a little actress there. A few months ago an Italian soprano had taken his fancy. Barbara had never let it show that any of them bothered her, but she had been relieved when the pretty songstress had flown away home. Lovely Signora Carlotti had been a worthy rival.

Now lesser mortals were aspiring to fill the soprano's place. Lady Goodrich had been risibly unsubtle in her pursuit at Vauxhall and Verity Marchant was constantly bumping her buxom hips against him.

In retaliation Barbara had taken a particular fancy to a few handsome gallants who danced attendance upon her. She had conducted discreet affairs—she knew Mark would not tolerate being the object of ridicule. But, if he had been jealous of those young gentlemen, he had admirably concealed it.

Nevertheless Barbara had always been sure that she held the key to Mark's heart, no matter their trifling peccadilloes. He might dally elsewhere, but she was the constant in his life and she had been confident that he would eventually make her his wife. Now she was frightened that her dearest ambition had been snatched from her grasp.

She flattened her back against the wall, her face a mask of shock and fury. She had not witnessed all that had gone on between Mark and Emily Beaumont on the terrace, but she had seen and heard enough to understand that she was losing him. She had glimpsed with her own eyes the kisses, the tenderness bestowed by her lover on another woman. And then the little trollop had mentioned a child! Emily Beaumont must believe herself to be increasing with Mark's bastard! And, from Mark's loving attitude towards the scheming hussy, Barbara guessed he might ask Miss Beaumont to marry him!

Barbara felt her back teeth grind in rage and frustration. She had hoped that *she* might conceive. She knew Mark well enough to realise that he would cherish and protect his firstborn, and the child's mother. But he had always been careful to let the sheets, or her belly, catch his seed, thus far denying her the right to his family and his name. Now that sly minx would usurp her place as his wife. Barbara dashed away the wrathful tears stinging her eyes and stiffened her spine. She was not about to put paid to years of devotion to Mark Hunter. He was hers and she would keep him!

Barbara glanced swiftly about the deserted room and noticed that a young fellow was wandering about, peering here and there, as though searching for someone. She thought she recognised him and, as he turned her way, a smile tilted her lips. It was Miss Beaumont's loyal puppy. He had been escorting Emily earlier and giving her moon-eyed looks. No doubt he was in pursuit of her just as she was in pursuit of Mark. In a flash of inspiration she recollected his name was Stephen Bond and his grandmother was Augusta, a friend of their hostess.

Barbara stepped over to Stephen and gave him a bright smile. Her fan was theatrically employed to cool her flushed face. 'It is so hot, is it not? I expect you slipped away from the concert to get some air. I did too.'

A neutral smile and a polite nod were his response. Stephen made to move on to look elsewhere for Emily.

'Might I ask you to accompany me to the terrace, Mr Bond?' Without awaiting a reply, Barbara attached her hand to the crook of his arm. 'I expect we will both benefit from a little night air.'

Stephen grimaced in barely concealed annoyance—it was the second time that evening that a woman, not of his choosing, had urged him to act as her escort. But he was too much of a gentleman to refuse. His frustration was limited to a terse, muttered agreement. An angry blush stained his fair cheeks as he allowed Barbara to steer him towards the terrace. As they approached the doors his misgivings increased. He looked askance at her. Without apparent cause she had suddenly burst into shrill laughter.

Barbara had a very good reason for creating a din. It was her intention to alert her faithless lover to her presence. She didn't want anyone else to witness that he was paying ardent attention to another woman. Especially not this fellow! Were Stephen Bond of a jealous, fiery nature—Barbara took a glance at him and curled a smile at the improbability—a rumpus might ensue and then her humiliation would become common knowledge.

Her loud giggling had the desired effect. With a groaned oath Mark gently put Emily from him and, threading her arm formally through his, began to lead her back towards the drawing-room doors. They were a few paces away from the light when Stephen and Barbara appeared on the terrace.

'Emily! There you are. Are you not well?' Stephen asked in concern, immediately quitting Barbara's side.

'I...just felt a little hot,' Emily explained with a strained smile. 'I'm better now.'

'That is good,' Barbara said sweetly. 'I have some salts you may borrow if you think it might help.'

Emily gave a quick shake of her head and murmured thanks.

'If you are a little feverish, you ought to hurry inside, Miss Beaumont, in case you take a chill.' Barbara gravely advised. 'Besides, I expect your mother has missed you too. She will have been imagining all sorts of odd things to be responsible for your absence.'

Emily avoided Mark's eyes as she joined Stephen. She had gone with Mark to the terrace determined that she would not again succumb to his skilful flirtation. Yet he had easily brushed aside her principles and her inhibitions and started to seduce her.

Just a short while ago she had criticised Tarquin for jeopardising her family's reputation. Yet had she not acted with equal disregard for decency? She had known very well that Mark was spoken for. She had also known that his mistress was close by, yet still she had let him kiss and caress her.

And how very firmly attached he was too! Emily had obliquely observed Barbara glide to Mark's side, then curl white fingers possessively over an elegant dark arm.

'Thank you, Mr Hunter, for your kind escort,' Emily said with stiff formality, and guilt writhing in the pit of her stomach.

'You're very welcome to it, Miss Beaumont,' Mark returned easily. His eyes rested for a long moment on Stephen, making the young man shift rather uncomfortably.

When Emily pulled gently on Stephen's arm to indicate it was time to go inside, her escort's relief was obvious enough to tug a side of Mark's mouth into a smile.

'Where have you been hiding this evening, Miss Beaumont?' Augusta Bond raised her lorgnette and peered shrewdly at Emily. 'You missed some good music, you know.'

'Emily was taking the air on the terrace, with Mr Hunter, Grandmama.' Stephen had answered after a short pause, for Emily seemed to be in a daze that had deepened a dent between her delicate brows.

'Ah…' Augusta said, and gave a significant nod. Her gimlet eyes shifted behind the glass to the people just entering the room. Barbara Emerson had a fierce determined smile on her face as she looked at her lover. Augusta was not fooled. It was not simply that the gentleman looked detached, and had his eyes on Emily. Augusta could easily tell when a woman was worried that she was about to be pensioned off. She had been cast aside herself by gentlemen friends before Mr Bond had swept her up the aisle.

'I'm sorry, Mrs Bond…did you say the concert was enjoyable?' Emily babbled, for she had sensed Mark's presence in the room, and his eyes on her.

'I did. And I'll also say that I had a notion you might do better for yourself than Nicholas Devlin.' The old lady had lowered her voice to add that. She gave Emily a subtle smile. 'I should like a glass of champagne. I think you deserve some, too, miss.' Augusta turned to her grandson. 'Miss Beaumont and I are off to have a chat to Fiona before the orchestra starts up again. Fiona knows all the latest gossip and I must have something to tell them back in Bath.'

'Are you soon going home, ma'am?' Emily

asked, desperately polite, as she tried to concentrate on anything at all other than what had occurred on the terrace with the imposing gentleman they were about to pass.

'I'm not sure when to leave,' Augusta replied. 'But before I go, I'd like to see Stephen happy.'

'Yes, of course…' Emily frowned and stole a glance at Augusta's profile. 'You think he is unhappy, ma'am?'

'Indeed, I do. And he always will be while he hankers after you,' Augusta said bluntly. 'You're a nice gel, Miss Beaumont, but you're not right for my grandson.'

'What a fine evening it was to be sure. Even the presence of that vinegar-faced Violet Pearson could not ruin my enjoyment.' Penelope slipped off her shawl and did a little twirl on the rug. 'Our hostess spent far more time talking to us than the Pearsons.' A wicked smile animated Penelope's face. 'We have Augusta to thank for being so favoured, and for making Violet so obviously *furious*.'

Emily gave her mother a smile and sat down in a chair in the parlour. They had not long ago arrived home. All Emily desired now was to sleep. Her head ached from her efforts to either make sense of the troubles that rotated dizzily in her mind, or banish them completely. Her eyes felt hot and weary. But her mother was eager to talk, for she had very much enjoyed their outing, and it would be churlish to deny her a brief résumé of gowns, gossip and guests.

'Well, I do think you could show a little more enthusiasm, Emily.' Penelope had guessed that her daughter was keen to retire. 'Lady Gerrard seemed to like you very much. And so did her nephew. I saw Stephen give him a scowl when he twice asked you to dance.' Penelope chuckled. 'It will not hurt Stephen to know he has a rival. Although I'm not sure the Brettles have as much money as one would expect for people related to the Gerrard clan.'

'It was all very pleasant indeed,' Emily said with a fleeting smile. 'I'm quite tired, Mama. I think I'll go up, for I can hardly keep my eyes open.'

Penelope shrugged and pouted in disappointment. 'Oh, by the by, where did you get to during the concert?'

'I was on the terrace…getting some air…I told you,' Emily said quietly.

'Ah, so you did. You were with Tarquin's friend, Mr Hunter.' Penelope gave a sigh. 'I expect you were trying to find out what he has discovered about the rogue. Must you tell me anything?' she asked in a martyred tone. 'I know your papa has no news of him at all.'

Emily felt her heart slow to a painful thud. She had hoped to avoid any mention of Tarquin, for she didn't want to lie. Stubbornly she clung to a forlorn hope that a mistake might have been made. Perhaps things were not as bad as they seemed, and she would do anything rather than unnecessarily upset her parents with a false alarm. 'Mr Hunter has not finished his investigations, Mama. We will know more soon, I'm sure.' With a murmured 'good night', Emily quickly slipped from the room.

Chapter Ten

'I think you owe me profuse thanks...but I will settle for a full account of what went on.'

Sarah had teasingly uttered that as soon as Mrs Beaumont closed the parlour door behind her. Moments before they had all enjoyed tea and ginger cake, whilst savouring every aspect of Lady Gerrard's magnificent party. But Penelope had now quit the room so the young ladies might enjoy a private cose.

Emily sent her friend a repressive look as she laid aside her napkin.

Undeterred, Sarah continued to grin mischievously at her whilst collecting spicy crumbs from her plate. 'I've been dying to know...did he kiss you?' She popped a sticky finger in her mouth.

Emily's cheeks grew rosy but she managed an insouciant little chuckle. 'I take it you are referring to my walk on the terrace with Mr Hunter last night.'

'Of course! It was good of me to divert Stephen, was it not?' Sarah arched an eyebrow. 'You did not seem put out to be left alone with Mark. I don't think you take against him as much as you would have me believe,' she slyly added.

Emily had mixed feelings about that! But it was true that she owed Sarah her thanks for having commandeered Stephen. Hot on the heels of that thought came another that made her ruefully acknowledge she was a coward. She would rather still be in blissful ignorance of her brother's calamitous *mésalliance*, and her own shameful behaviour.

'What happened?' Sarah insisted on knowing. 'That's the second time I've noticed Mark Hunter pay you particular attention. And he gives you the most smouldering looks. I wish a rich, handsome bachelor would stare at me like that.'

'You would not if you knew his reasons,' Emily returned pithily and then regretted having further whetted her friend's curiosity.

'Did he take shocking liberties with you in the dark? I've heard he's a rakish character.' Sarah settled comfortably into the sofa, eyes round as saucers. She shivered, massaged at gooseflesh on her arms.

'What did he do...say?' Sarah persisted with her inquisition. 'Is he angling to pay court, do you think?'

'Don't be a henwit! You know very well that Mr Hunter is already spoken for.' Emily scolded lightly. 'He spent more time at his mistress's side than he did at mine.'

'Perhaps he did. But his eyes were on you most of the while. And I'm sure she knew it,' Sarah said with a gleeful chuckle. 'I doubt you'll be receiving an invitation to Mrs Emerson's soirées!'

'Well, that's a relief!' Emily muttered seriously. The thought of attending a salon hosted by Mark's mistress made her feel quite ill.

'We are friends! You must have something a bit outrageous to tell me.'

'If I did, it would concern Tarquin.' Emily gave her friend a rueful look. 'There is only one reason Mr Hunter and I need to converse in private, to discuss my troublesome brother! They are friends, and Mark has been good enough to try to find out what the miscreant is now up to.'

Sarah looked genuinely disappointed at that explanation. 'You don't think he might be more interested in you than your brother?'

Emily flapped a hand, outwardly dismissing the notion as absurd. But she averted her face to shield her expression. Although Mark had declared he wanted nothing from her for his services as detective, it seemed that he always did get a sensual reward…and with very little coaxing…

Sarah sank back into the cushions, contemplating her clasped hands, her mood now oddly subdued.

Emily took the opportunity to steer the conversation to another gentleman. 'Thank you for keeping Stephen company yesterday.'

'Oh, I didn't mind at all,' Sarah glanced up. 'In fact…' A grimace turned up her snub nose and she simply shrugged.

'Go on,' Emily gently prompted. It had never before occurred to her that Sarah might hold a torch for Stephen.

'It doesn't matter,' Sarah muttered.

'I think it does,' Emily countered softly.

'I just think Stephen is very nice,' Sarah self-consciously admitted whilst twirling a chestnut curl about a finger. 'And if I thought he might stop vainly pining for you…for I know you will never want him…I might tell him so and see what happens.' She clucked her tongue. 'How daft I must sound! You are blonde and beautiful and I am dark and plain.'

'You are *not* plain, you are pretty!' Emily stressed. 'You are younger than me by three years, and have a fine complexion. You never blush an ugly red as I do. Brunettes are the rage this season, too,' she added with an emphatic nod.

Sarah seemed deaf to her friend's compliments. 'Besides, if Stephen gave up the chase so easily, when he is obviously in love with you, he wouldn't be nice at all, would he?' she reasoned.

'Yes, he would!' Emily forcefully begged to differ. 'He would be a fickle character and not to be trusted.'

'I don't think Stephen loves me. It is an infatuation. And we all are entitled to be in thrall to that, at least once.' Emily gave her friend a twinkling smile.

'Are you hinting that I have an infatuation for Stephen?' Sarah asked, rather sharply.

'No! I am saying that I understand how easily one might confuse the two emotions, for I believe I did. For a long time I thought I truly loved Viscount Devlin. Now I am not sure whether it was love or infatuation. I know I found the idea of being in love very appealing, perhaps very deluding too…'

'You don't know how it feels to be in love?'

About to answer in the negative, Emily hesitated—her mind had veered to the memory of being enclosed in Mark's protective embrace. That recollection led to another: the sensation of a sultry warm mouth moving on hers and firm, confident fingers arousing her body. 'I'm not sure,' Emily blurted, her cheeks pink.

It seemed too absurd that she had immediately associated a gentleman she didn't know very well, or like very much, with love. But perhaps she *was* coming to know Mark, an inner voice whispered, and perhaps because of that she *didn't* dislike him as much as once she had. Heaven only knew he had been of immense help so far in piecing together the puzzle surrounding Tarquin's disappearance. It would be an ingrate indeed who would still disapprove of a gentleman who had gone to so much trouble for her family.

'Perhaps Stephen is not wasting his time waiting for you, then,' Sarah said stiffly, having stabbed a guess at the identity of the fellow occupying her friend's thoughts. 'Please forget I told you I liked him, which I do, of course, but not in *that* way. I would not want you to think you have a rival, or that I was presumptuous.'

'I was not thinking of Stephen just now. He is not the one…that is… Oh! Don't be like that, Sarah,' Emily pleaded as her friend got quickly to her feet.

'I must be going,' Sarah said tightly. 'I told Mama

I would accompany her to Baldwin's for some velvet.' With no more ado she stepped briskly to the parlour door and quit the room.

Emily felt quite melancholy as she walked with her friend to the vestibule. A tension now existed between her and Sarah and yet there had been no real disagreement between them, just talk of gentlemen. As Emily watched her friend descend the steps and turn towards home, without a backward glance, she sighed and wondered if finding a husband was really as beneficial as their mothers would have them believe.

Sarah Harper was not the only young woman who was, that morning, despondent in the knowledge that a gentleman did not reciprocate her feelings.

Barbara Emerson had just received a message from her maid that Mr Hunter had called and was waiting below. Mark never waited below. He had for many years visited her at this house and, whatever the hour, had felt comfortable coming to her boudoir. Whether he arrived to talk or to make love, he never before had stood on ceremony. Now he did, and she feared she knew why.

She had been aware for a while that his ardour was cooling. When he had brought her home last night, despite her best efforts to lure him indoors, he had gone off without even giving her a proper kiss.

Before Claudine's gaze darted away, Barbara had seen the mingling of pity and embarrassment in the girl's eyes. Even her French maid knew Barbara was about to be cast off. She trusted Claudine to be loyal and discreet, but soon it would be all over town that she was no longer Mark's mistress, or his future wife. Speculation would start as to who had usurped her, but they would not guess. Only she knew the identity of the brazen hussy who had stolen Mark away.

Barbara paced to and fro, her face set in rigid lines, her lacy negligee sailing out from her voluptuous body with the vigour of her movement. She could plead an indisposition. Of course he would not believe her, for not once had she refused him an audience. Either he would leave or he would relent and come up to find her. And then she might be able to use her wiles to stop the awful words in his throat, before he could utter them.

'*Madame* is indisposed, sir.' The petite maid peeped at a hard, dark face, then quickly her eyes sought the floor.

'In that case, convey my commiserations to *ma-*

dame,' Mark said quietly. 'And tell her I will return tomorrow.'

If Mark was aware that he was being observed from between the curtains in the window above, he gave no sign. Springing aboard his curricle, he set the fine animals to a trot. His flinty demeanour was not caused by the woman he anticipated might not gracefully accept he no longer wanted her, but by the friend who was creating havoc in the lives of so many people.

With an effort he banished Tarquin, and his exquisite…captivating…sister from his mind and forced himself to concentrate on what was to be done to make the break with Barbara as painless as possible. If she continued to try to delay the inevitable by refusing to see him, then he would send her a note. But that seemed the coward's way and he would sooner act honourably. He didn't want to hurt her, but neither could he continue to condone her fantasy that they had a future together.

After Barbara's husband had died, and they had resumed their affair, he had bluntly told her that he could not again promise her his fidelity or his love. There had been a tacit understanding between them that he would want his liberty, and from time to time, other women. He had appreciated that Barbara was too proud to nag him over those liaisons. For his part, he had never mentioned those *special* gallants who escorted her home, then discreetly slipped out in the small hours.

Despite their passing fancies, they had continued to share mutual pleasure, and Mark had not previously wanted to put an end to something that suited them both. But lately her hints that they should marry were becoming less subtle and were apt to grate on his nerves. She had become disturbingly possessive, and kept him under surveillance when they were out. He knew it was not a coincidence that she had come on to the terrace at Lady Gerrard's. She had probably been stalking him for a while before she showed herself. His tolerance of it all was spent, and he realised that his desire for her was too.

To safeguard fond memories, and Barbara's dignity, he had hoped to end it without rancour. Mark sent a rueful look skyward. Worthy sentiment…but would he be as determined to act with such ruthless efficiency if it wasn't for the matter of Miss Emily Beaumont?

Emily knew of his long-standing relationship with Barbara, and he imagined she deemed him a faithless rogue. But she still responded to him sweetly, despite her misgivings, and he was encouraged to believe she might yet grow fond of him.

Stolen kisses were one thing, but she would shun his formal courtship unless he honestly declared Barbara was out of his life. His smile turned wry as he realised he was gratified to know Emily considered Barbara her rival. And she did; he had noticed a decidedly antagonistic glint in her silver eyes as Barbara had made her appearance on the terrace with Stephen Bond. That conceit caused Mark to choke a laugh. Of course it was possible the cause of her pique was seeing her beau escorting another woman.

Musing darkly on that particular admirer—a fellow who had done nothing to merit uncharitable thoughts—made Mark grudgingly acknowledge he was jealous. Stephen Bond had a *tendresse* for Emily. Tarquin had told him so some months previously. His friend had also helpfully imparted the news that Emily liked the fellow, but was not expected to accept his proposal even if, at some time, Mr Bond found the temerity to issue it. Stephen was beneath his grandmother's thumb. The woman held the purse strings, and her grandson's inheritance, in her grasp.

With that thought encouraging him, Mark flicked the reins over the greys' backs, urging them to a faster pace. His concentration returned to Emily's brother. It was high time he had a few strong words with Tarquin, and he had a good idea where he might find him.

Emily restlessly paced the floor of her chamber. She had been feeling odd since Sarah had left. Although she could settle on nothing specific that she had said or done wrong to cause a rift with Sarah, none the less a pang of guilt would not be banished. With a final tug of the brush through her thick hair she tossed it, in a glint of silver, on to the bed. Aimlessly she went to the dressing chest and peered in the glass at her reflection.

Large silver eyes darted from pert nose to wide mouth to sharp little chin. She frowned as though she might find the answers she sought in her features. Was she being cruel to Stephen? She certainly liked him…but as a friend. Would she ever accept being a true wife to him? Bearing his children? Perhaps if he knew how she felt he might declare her a fraud, and their friendship a sham.

Augusta Bond knew the truth. Since the woman had first met her she had been adamant that she was not right for her grandson. Did Augusta consider her a heartless tease? She didn't want to hurt Stephen any more than she had wanted to upset her friend Sarah.

With a sigh Emily tipped the glass away from her and went to the door. She *had* been selfish in keeping Stephen dangling on a string...*in reserve*, her mother would put it, in case no better bachelor could be found to take her from the shelf. It was time to set him free to make an attachment with someone else...someone like Sarah.

'I was hoping to bump into you again, miss.'

Emily spun about at that sibilant hiss to see Mickey Riley peering in her direction from a nearby shop doorway. Once certain that she had noticed him, and in a scene that Emily felt she had played out before, he sloped nonchalantly along the pavement a yard or two, then darted into an alley.

After a moment Emily followed him, her expression grim.

Although she had hoped to quickly deliver the letter in her pocket to Stephen, it was opportune that Riley had accosted her. She would dearly love to give him a piece of her mind! She suspected that Tarquin's marriage had not been an unlucky aberration, but had been plotted in advance. It might not have come about but for this avaricious fellow.

'We ought to stop meeting like this, Mr Riley,' Emily said with harsh sarcasm.

Riley's lips pulled into a sideways grin. 'I'm flattered yer took the trouble to find out me name.'

'Please don't be. It was no trouble at all,' Emily returned icily. 'I do know who you are and much more about you besides.'

Riley cocked an insolent eyebrow at her, daring her to voice what she knew.

'You go first, and make it quick.' Emily crossed her arms over her waist in a display of impatience. 'I have no intention of spending more than a minute or two with you.'

'Well, that's a fine way to greet a feller who's been stood around hoping to give yer some news about yer brother.'

'I already have some news about my brother, Mr Riley,' Emily snapped in an underbreath. 'Believe me, I would rather not know it. So, if you are about to tell me that he has been coerced to wed one of your…' Emily swallowed the vulgarity. 'One of your female associates,' she resumed stiltedly, 'you may save your breath.'

'So you found out about Jenny, did yer?' Riley cupped his stubbly jaw in a hand and glanced at her from beneath lowered lids. His devious mind turned over recent events. He came to the swift conclusion that Mark Hunter had relayed to Miss Beaumont the unsavoury news. In which case that gentleman and this lady were *very* close. It was hardly a topic of light conversation. Riley had thought that if Mark Hunter were to babble to anyone about it he would have chosen old man Beaumont. Mickey gave his chin a final tickle. He'd need to tread carefully if he was to successfully play all sides against the middle or he'd risk losing a tidy profit.

With a careless gesture he said, 'Now yer know why I was keen to find Tarquin. Don't fret now. There's a way to square it afore all hell breaks loose.' He gave her a sympathetic smile. ''Course yer won't want to worry yer ma and pa with it all. But keeping it quiet and putting it right'll cost.' Riley snaked his tongue over his lips.

'And how exactly are you going to put it right?'

'Well, now—that's for me to know, and for you to pay to find out, ain't it?'

Emily gave a little scornful laugh. 'You fool! Are you about to ask for payment for a silly scheme to pretend the marriage didn't take place? Jeremiah Plumb performed the service and is a bona fide clergyman, so I understand. What will you do? Bribe him to delete the records and in doing so embroil my brother in yet more trouble?'

Mickey gave her a startled glare.

'It *was* your intention to do that, wasn't it?' Emily said with quiet incredulity.

'You think you're pretty clever, don't yer, miss?' Riley hissed. 'But that ain't what I wanted to speak to you about, although it do concern your brother.' Mickey felt cheated. He had thought his plot quite ingenious, yet it had taken her no more than a few minutes to unravel it.

When he had set out today he had been unsure whether to go ahead with the Viscount's wicked plan to entrap this lovely young lady for his own base needs. Now he thought it might serve her right. She could do with taking down a peg or two.

'Tell me quickly what it is, then,' Emily demanded. 'I have an important letter to deliver.'

'I've got a message for you from your brother.' Mickey jutted his chin. He'd got her attention now! An immediate gleam of concern had widened her eyes. He held out a hand. 'Crown'll do it.' Mickey felt a sense of triumph that the little madam was paying him for her ruination. His fingers sprang like a trap over the coin that Emily had furiously slapped there. 'Yer brother sent Jenny a note and off we went to see where he's holed up. He's got no money, so it were pointless looking to *him* to square Plumb and give me a little consideration for me efforts.' A sneer curled Mickey's top lip. It was the truth. He had certainly wasted his time with the loser. 'He's been drinking too much and sleeping rough since he bolted. Now he's taken a chill and it's turned nasty.' Mickey slipped a look at Emily to see her reaction to the tale so far. He could tell she was anxious to hear more. 'Jenny reckons all he needs is a dose of summat, and a hot meal inside of him, and he'll be good as new.' Mickey shook his head in a show of exasperation. 'Yer brother's fretting he might turn up his toes, and wants to see you. But he don't want to see yer pa just yet 'cos he's ashamed…naturally.'

'Why did *Jenny* not come to see me sooner?' Emily wailed in a stifled tone.

'*I* take care of things where Jenny's concerned,' Riley stated threateningly. 'Anyhow, it were only a day or two ago we got wind of it all.' He gave her a fierce look. 'Yer brother made it clear he only wants to see you. If you turn up with anyone else, he won't show his face.'

Emily's complexion was now quite ashen with strain. 'Are you lying? Is this a ruse to extort more money from me?'

'I could've arst fer more just now, miss,' Riley

pointed out, adopting a pious look. 'And I don't want to see him push up the daisies any more'n you do.'

'He'd be no use then, would he?' Emily breathed furiously. Riley might have scoffed at Tarquin's impecunious state, but Emily was sure the villain had not yet given up hope of finding a profit in her brother's calamitous marriage. 'Tell me at once where he is.'

'I've got a rig. A jarvey won't be keen to go that far. Be quicker 'n' cheaper if I take you. Won't arouse suspicion with yer parents if you're there 'n' back double quick.'

Emily cast a look at her feet; her head was feeling dizzy with milling anxieties. Riley was right on one score. Hiring a vehicle and driver would be costly, and take time. If he was telling the truth, and Tarquin was ill, she needed to see him immediately, and try to talk some sense into the dolt. It was inevitable that he must return home and face the music, ashamed or not, if he was to get better. Slowly she nodded, whilst prevaricating, 'I can't go right now. I need to get something from the apothecary for Tarquin. There is a potion that calms fever. I will meet you later this afternoon.'

Emily did not for a moment trust Riley, and was nervous about going anywhere alone with him. She urgently needed assistance, and there was only one person to turn to…Mark Hunter…

Chapter Eleven

'**M**r Hunter is out, Miss Beaumont.' Such was the butler's polite response when Emily gave her name and requested an immediate audience with his master.

Geoffrey Lomax cast a dubious eye over the lovely young woman. It was obvious that she was a lady of good class, and that made her behaviour the more bizarre. It was not at all proper for an unaccompanied spinster to pay an impromptu call on a bachelor. His stern look softened a mite as he noticed her downcast expression. He deduced it was a matter of vital importance that had made her act bold and look glum. 'If you would like to leave a message for Mr Hunter, I will make sure he has it directly he returns,' he promised.

Chaotic thoughts cluttered her brain, keeping Emily wide-eyed and mute before the manservant. What was she to do? In a short while she was to meet Riley, and he had made it clear he would not wait if she were late for their rendezvous. But she desperately wanted Mark apprised of this latest development. Trusting Riley to his word carried a grave risk to her personal safety. The matter was too confidential to leave a verbal message with the butler, but a communication of some sort must be made. 'Might I beg leave to have a pen and paper in order to write your master a note?'

A nod and a smile from Lomax invited her in to Mark's mansion on Belgrave Crescent.

Emily stepped over the threshold and into a vast hallway. Absently her mind registered its opulence; smooth flags on the floor were of the same pristine marble as the graceful pillars that soared out of sight. Whilst the butler disappeared to fetch writing implements for her, she noted the stark elegance of Mark Hunter's home. She paced nervously, oblivious to being surreptitiously observed from outside.

When Barbara's equipage had drawn up at the kerb a few minutes ago, she had been immensely frustrated to see Emily hurrying up the wide stone steps. She had been on the point of using them herself!

She had swallowed her pride, and her fears that she might be hastening her own demise, to come to see Mark. Her hope had been to find him in a mellow mood and thus receptive to sharing sweet reminiscences of their youth. Barbara's scowl deepened. The sight of the Beaumont girl had shaken her optimism, seeded doubts that Mark might be swayed by appeals to his memory…or his virility.

The footman closed the huge doors, cutting off Barbara's view of Emily, thereby prompting a few unladylike expletives to roll off her tongue. She slammed her back against the squabs. It seemed that Miss Beaumont was soliciting Mark's attention without so much as a maid in tow as token chaperon. But there was little satisfaction in knowing that her rival was a brazen baggage.

A furrow marred her brow as she sought for a reason why Emily might act with such audacity. Barbara was still ruminating on that conundrum when she heard the door again being opened. Quickly she shifted forward on the seat and twitched aside the blind. She watched as Emily descended the steps and headed off at a fast pace.

A smile curled Barbara's tinted lips for Emily's countenance had been puckered with strain. Perhaps Mark had been disgusted by her shocking intrusion and had sent her off with a flea in her ear. She had not been inside the house above ten minutes.

Assisted by a footman, Barbara was soon out of her carriage and mounting the steps.

'Mr Hunter is not at home, Mrs Emerson.' Mr Lomax coupled the information with a dour expression. He had never warmed to this woman despite knowing she had, for many years, retained her position as the master's favourite lady friend. His lids descended over eyes studying Barbara's lush figure swathed in muslin and a flimsy silk cape. Obviously the woman had attractions…if no sense on how to keep warm on a chilly day. And Mr Hunter was certainly a red-blooded gentleman.

Barbara sailed past Lomax and into the house with all the pomp of a woman who believed it her right to do so. She twirled about and gave the butler a perfunctory smile. 'How disagreeable to have missed him. But he was not expecting me, so I cannot scold him.' Her features were a study of insouciance as she glanced about. Her dark eyes darted back to a piece of parchment resting on an ebony surface. Idly Barbara moved in that direction to check her appearance in a gilt-framed mirror positioned over the console table. Her bonnet ribbons were loosened, then made more secure, but all the while covert glances were scanning what she now recognised to be a letter. On it she could decipher Mark's name, and it had undoubtedly been written in a female hand. Barbara's heart jumped a beat, for she had noticed something that indicated it could be from only one woman: the ink was still moist! Swiftly she turned her back on her reflection and re-garded Lomax, but her hands were gripping the edge of the table behind her.

Her mind was suddenly overwhelmed by the whispered words she had overheard on Lady Ger-rard's terrace. *But what if there is a child...what are we to do then?* Did Emily Beaumont now know for certain she was increasing with Mark's child? Such staggering news would certainly prompt her to dis-regard etiquette and urgently seek him. And she *had* looked violently troubled when she left this house a short while ago.

Barbara's fingers tightened on ebony as she strove to contain her tormented imaginings. 'I shall not leave a message and you need not tell Mr Hunter that I called.'

Mr Lomax elevated a quizzical eyebrow. 'As you wish, ma'am.'

Barbara's exploring fingers located paper and snatched. Suddenly she surged towards the door, rapidly covering marble in small steps. 'I think that is all,' she said as she swept past Mr Lomax. A regal nod at the footman bid he attend the door.

'Does your wife know what you get up to?'

The drawled irony made Tarquin shoot up out of the armchair. The young woman who had been balancing astride his lap tumbled awkwardly sideways. She quickly scrambled to her feet whilst smoothing down her skirts and giving Tarquin's arm an admonishing thump for such rough treatment.

'What in damnation…?' Tarquin's unshaven jaw dropped to his chest. Agitatedly he scraped his fingers through his lank, flaxen hair, all the while gawping at Mark. 'You just gave me the fright of my life, Hunter. What in damnation are *you* doing here?' he snarled, fumbling at his breeches, his face ruddy with embarrassment.

'What am *I* doing here?' Mark echoed in a tone replete with sarcasm. He looked about the comfortable, if spartanly furnished, room. 'Last time I saw the deeds I owned this lodge. I thus feel quite entitled to use it. More to the point, Beaumont, is what the hell you are doing here. Besides worrying the life out of your family, of course. But then I suppose you've not given much thought to any of that, have you?'

'I hope you're not going to preach,' Tarquin muttered. 'You're no saint by any means.'

'True; nevertheless you need a lesson over this.' Mark moved purposefully closer, but halted when Tarquin's companion skipped to shield him with her dishevelled figure. She continued to button her bodice, but up went her chin, and she challengingly met Mark's eyes.

A contemptuous look was directed over her head at Tarquin before Mark strolled away to examine what was on the small dining table. He picked up a fork and turned over the remnants of a half-eaten meal of cheese and venison. A bottle of claret had a small amount left in it. Mark recognised the wine as from his cellar—a particularly good vintage— and it prompted him to wryly smile and wonder what provisions, if any, were left in the store. Mark poured what remained of the claret into a tumbler and tossed it back in a gulp. As he replaced his glass he remarked drily, 'I see you've not gone without…' A significant glance lingered on the woman. 'Does your wife care that you've abandoned her? Or perhaps the honeymoon is already over.'

'This *is* my wife,' Tarquin admitted petulantly, and flung himself down into the chair he'd recently vacated.

'Ah…I take it the honeymoon is progressing well, then.' Mark took a more interested look at the pretty young woman and realised he vaguely recognised her. If his memory served him correctly, he had spotted Riley and her loitering in the vicinity of the *modiste*'s shop on Regent Street. On that occasion she had been wearing a flamboyant hat that had shielded her features. 'Your manners are sadly lacking, Tarquin. Aren't you going to properly introduce us?'

Tarquin did so, tersely. He gained his feet with a sigh and ambled to stand by his wife's side in a show of grudging loyalty. Jenny slipped her hand through his arm and rewarded his gallantry with a little peck on the cheek. Mark received from her a glower that dared him to comment.

'I suppose my marriage is common knowledge if you've come here looking for me. No doubt my father is beside himself and Mother is prostrate on a sofa with her salts—'

'They don't know,' Mark cut sharply over Tarquin's self-pitying whine. 'And you had best give some serious thought to what you intend to do about the mess you're in.'

'He'll cut me off without a penny.'

'Can you blame him? You must have understood the risk you were taking.'

'I hardly understood a blasted thing! I was so far in my cups, I was barely conscious throughout the service.'

Irritably Tarquin shrugged off Jenny's possessive grip and stomped to a window of the hunting lodge. He gazed out through brown bars of bark to greensward in the distance. Finally he sighed and said, 'It's a God-awful mess. I don't know what to do.'

'You've got about half an hour to decide; then, ready or not, you're coming back with me.' Mark said in a voice that brooked no refusal. He glanced about. 'I'm afraid your sojourn enjoying all the comforts of home, at my expense, has just ended. And to make sure you fully understand that...I'll take back my spare keys.'

Tarquin turned his back on the pastoral view of Enfield Chase. Reluctantly he fished in a pocket, then lobbed metal on to the table. His mumbled gratitude for enjoying free hospitality was soon followed by, 'So if it is *not* common knowledge about my marriage, how did *you* find out?'

'Riley told me. He's been trying to use your *mésalliance* to extort money from Emily. I've no doubt he would have blackmailed you instead had he discovered where you were hiding.' Mark glanced at

Jenny. 'I take it your wife has *your* best interests at heart, not Riley's?'

Tarquin looked affronted at that but, nevertheless, shot a dubious look Jenny's way.

She had the grace to immediately blush. 'I tried to put him off going after your sister,' she insisted. 'I told him to forget all about the Beaumonts and find another punter who'd cough up easy. But he's a stubborn blighter. He wouldn't let it rest.' She raised doe-eyes to her husband. 'I could've let on to Mickey where you was hiding, but I never did… honest…'

'Emily's embroiled in this?' Tarquin had suddenly recaptured control of his shocked senses. His hoarse demand cut across his wife's reassurances. Her little nod sent both his hands to cup his face, and he shook his head in a show of remorse.

Jenny snuggled against him, said softly, 'I come here today to tell you about Riley and what he's up to now, 'cos it ain't right, and I want no part of it. I would've said sooner about your sister, but…' the pink in her cheeks deepened to crimson. '…you distracted me and it slipped me mind.'

Tarquin fidgeted on the spot. He couldn't deny he had given Jenny very little opportunity to strike up a conversation since she arrived about twenty minutes ago. He cleared his throat, asked stiffly, 'What have you to tell me about Emily?'

Jenny seemed suddenly tongue-tied. It was not the frowning look from her husband unsettling her, but the callous stare from his friend. Suddenly the fellow made a violently impatient gesture, making her jump and slip behind Tarquin.

'If you know that Riley is planning more mischief in order to extort money from Miss Beaumont…' Mark began.

'It isn't that,' she blurted. 'Mickey's getting paid all right, but not from her.' She looked at Tarquin apologetically. 'He's made a bargain with a fellow who's got a fancy for your sister, and wants a chance to be private with her. Mickey, the vile devil, is getting paid to set up a meeting between them.' Jenny quickly glanced away from the terrifying glint in Mark Hunter's eyes.

'What nonsense!' Tarquin snorted. 'I know Stephen Bond fancies Emily, but he's a decent fellow. He hasn't got it in him to plot a seduction, I'm sure of it.' He shot a look at Mark and paled, for his friend's features might have been hewn from stone.

'What arrangements has Riley made? How is he to lure her there? Is it to soon take place?' Mark fired the questions at Jenny.

Jenny blinked rapidly and moistened her lips. 'It's soon,' she admitted. 'I know Mickey wants to get his hands on the cash quick as can be. But that's all he's let on to me. By my reckoning he'll use Tarquin as the bait.'

'And who asked Mickey to set it up?' Mark demanded with icy quiet. 'And don't lie to me.'

Jenny simply gazed forlornly at Tarquin for support. But he seemed to have retreated into a daze. His thumbnail was being whittled away by worrying teeth.

'Tell me the name of the devil or by Heaven I'll throttle it out of you!' Mark gritted at Jenny through unmoving lips.

'Steady on, Hunter…' Tarquin snapped to attention to remonstrate on his wife's behalf.

'It's Devlin!' Jenny suddenly shouted with tears of fright sparking in her eyes. She knew that she had just burned her bridges by betraying Mickey. If he ever found out his money-spinner had turned sour due to her, he would not hesitate to seek revenge. She took a deep breath and repeated shakily, 'It's Devlin…that's who it is…the brute…'

Emily looked up at the façade of the house and frowned. Moments ago she had disembarked from

Riley's gig and now stood with him on gravel that formed a circular drive to an elegant double-fronted residence. She took a look about. The property was definitely isolated from its neighbours, but was of grand proportions, and that put it beyond Tarquin's pocket even had he been flush.

On the journey to the edge of town she had pondered on the hardship Tarquin might be enduring. Images of rural cottages with draughts whistling through windows and doors had beset her mind. She had feared she might find him a shivering wreck wrapped in rags with no fire in the grate. On looking skyward she could see curls of smoke drifting lazily upwards from twin chimneys.

Riley had told her that Tarquin was ill from sleeping rough. If he were within these doors, it would be more likely he was in fine fettle, and had been reposing on a feather bed at night.

She turned to Riley with a dubious frown and an unpleasant sensation gnawing at the pit of her stomach. 'Tarquin would never have the means to rent such a house. As far as I am aware he has no friends hereabouts who might let him use their property. Are you sure this is the right place?'

'It's the right place right enough,' Mickey returned on a bark of a laugh, but he avoided her eyes.

Suddenly he stooped and grabbed the little bag of provisions and potions she had brought with her. 'Come along, miss, won't do to dawdle or we'll never get back to town afore it gets dark.' As though to emphasise that threat he glanced up deliberately at the lowering clouds in the west.

Emily skipped after his striding figure despite the host of niggling suspicions in her mind. Before she could voice even one anxiety, the door was suddenly opened by a manservant. Emily hesitated, the hairs on the back of her neck stirring as she noted the fellow's neat uniform. It was an unusual livery of brown and gold that she recalled seeing before…quite recently. An instinct made Emily stop and take a pace back.

Riley had noticed her hesitation and, firmly clasping one of her elbows, propelled her up the steps and into the hallway. The manservant immediately closed the door and silently withdrew.

Emily spun about to gaze at Riley. But his attention was elsewhere.

'There…all ready and waiting,' he said, with a leer, but it was not her he was addressing in such a lewd tone of voice.

Slowly she became aware of approaching footfalls and twisted about. Her soft mouth slackened in amazement and her delicate brows pulled together. 'Nicholas?' She tested the name even though she could see quite clearly that it was indeed her former fiancé. She gave a little hysterical laugh. 'Oh, never say that *you* have given my brother shelter. I thought the two of you were still at odds. Do you know all about Tarquin's disappearance?'

'I'm afraid I don't, my dear, nor do I want to,' Devlin said bluntly. 'But over dinner you can tell me all about it, if you like. I'm prepared to indulge you, despite I couldn't give a tinker's cuss how he does. It's *you* who arouses my interest,' he concluded throatily.

Emily's soft lips slackened, her eyes grew round. An absurd notion that the two men might have been in cahoots to dupe her entered her mind and refused to budge.

'I take it this is mine?' Riley said and snatched up something from the hall table.

Emily whisked about to look at him, but was uncertain to what he referred. Then she heard the unmistakable chink of coins as they were dropped into his pocket.

Mickey Riley had been paid by Viscount Devlin to bring her here! Swiftly she strode to Nicholas and glared up into his tawny eyes. 'Have you plotted with this…this cur to trick me? Have you brought me here for no good reason?'

Nicholas put out a hand to touch her face soothingly. 'You're here for a very good reason, my love. I know you remember another such time when we were alone…and both so very pleased to be so. Soon you'll be glad I acted the despot.'

Emily savagely slapped away the fingers that stroked her cheek. 'You despicable beast!' She would have returned her fist to her side, but it spontaneously raised and made vicious contact with his jaw. Obliquely she heard Riley give a hoot of laughter.

Nicholas pressed a few fingers to the livid stain her assault had put on his skin.

'If it's taming you want tonight, I'll give it to you,' he said hoarsely, his eyes darkening with a mix of anger and excitement.

Emily felt fear painfully knotting her insides, but steeled her courage, determined not to panic. 'Was it not enough that you seduced me once before?' she whispered in a tone of sheer loathing.

'Of course not, or why would I go to such trouble and expense to do it again?' Nicholas tore his eyes from Emily's lovely features to give Riley a speaking look.

A ribald chuckle from Riley was the extent of

him taking his leave. The sound seemed to echo about the hallway, petrifying Emily for a moment. Quickly gathering her senses, she flew towards the open door to escape from the house but, from the shadows, the manservant appeared. The fellow turned the key in the lock and removed it. As Emily watched her gaoler disappear she remembered where she had before seen that distinctive earth-brown livery: it had been in Whiting Street. Devlin's coachman had been caped in brown and gold.

Her heart was thudding painfully slowly as she turned back to Devlin. She felt barely able to breathe let alone speak. Finally her arid, trembling lips formed brave words. 'You are a devil and I am utterly ashamed that I once knew so little about your character that I wanted to marry you.'

'Hush…' Devlin purred as he pursued her retreating figure until she was cornered. 'You have nothing to fear from me, Emily. I understand that you are angry at my scheming with that ghastly ruffian. But what could I do?' He shrugged elegant shoulders. 'You refused to meet me…sent me cruel letters spurning my love. Why? I want nothing from you that you have not before freely given.'

Chapter Twelve

⁓⊸⟩⟨⊷⁓

'I'll swing for Devlin! I should have finished him off last time!' The dangerous sentiment exploded from Tarquin as Mark's curricle ground to a halt outside the Beaumont residence in Callison Crescent.

As they had sped through the northern suburbs of town Mark had been similarly plagued by murderous thoughts. But he had kept tightly leashed his emotions and his threats. For now, saving Emily was his only concern. Once that was achieved he would be ready to turn his mind to retribution…

'Devlin will pay.' It was a vow as cold and hard as a knife thrust. 'You may stake your life on it. But for now we must ensure Emily is warned of the dangers.'

Tarquin sprang to the ground, his features contorted with anguish and remorse. Mark knew his friend was concerned not only for the safety of his sister but for his wife too.

About half an hour ago Jenny had been set down. Shortly before she had disembarked, she had voiced her fear that Mickey would exact revenge if he discovered she had ruined his deal with Devlin. But she had bravely reassured Tarquin that she would lie low with an aunt who lived in Hackney until things could be sorted out. And there, in Brewer Street, they had left her.

'Your wife is right in one respect,' Mark said. 'Riley doesn't yet know you have returned to your family. If he tries to use your absence to lure Emily away, the trick is exposed for what it is.'

The grooves about Tarquin's mouth deepened as he manfully strove to conceal his distress. He had set in motion a disastrous sequence of events and the consequences were coming home to roost. Mark saw Tarquin's lips tighten, but felt not a twinge of pity for him. Emily was his only concern; once he knew for certain she was safe, Tarquin would be the second target for his wrath.

'It might be wise to keep the worst of it all from your parents,' Mark suggested tightly. 'Their natural outrage might create a hue and cry and give the miscreants time to skedaddle or concoct a defence.'

'There's nowhere that cur can hide that I won't find him.'

'I'll deal with the Viscount.'

Tarquin cuffed his dewy nose, then paced restlessly back and forth on the pavement. 'You may go and batter the fiend if you like, but it won't stop me killing him afterwards! I had him for a callous libertine, but not so low that he would scheme to ruin a gentlewoman he once purported to adore!' Abruptly he stalked off towards the house, but Mark called him back.

'What caused you to fight him all those years ago? Did your hatred spring from the broken engagement between Emily and Devlin?'

Tarquin shook his head and gazed fiercely into the dusk. 'The engagement was broken *after* I gave him a beating, not before.' He paused, shifted his weight from foot to foot. 'I've never told Emily this—or my parents for that matter. Emily, especially, would be mortified to know what sort of vile character she'd once loved. She was upset for months after their betrothal ended.' He gave Mark a piercing look. 'If my father had found out he would have called for pistols. But I trust you to keep this to yourself.' His unshaven chin was cradled in fidgeting fingers. 'In my opinion the Viscount was relieved the betrothal came to nought. He was a fortune hunter, and Emily's dowry was never going to be enough to satisfy his greed, or his debts.' Tarquin's expression turned sheepish. 'You probably think I've got a devil of a nerve to talk so about a fellow's gambling debts, but I would never sell my soul, or betray a woman's love, for cash.' He plunged his hands into his pockets. 'Anyhow, on one long night in White's, when we both had been several hours at the faro table, I took a short break. He didn't know I'd returned and was close behind him. I overheard him boasting about Emily to one of his cronies…lewd disrespectful talk…about how fortunate he was that his betrothed was a hot wanton, as though already he had bedded her.' Tarquin drew in a sharp breath. 'He was drunk, it's true, but there was no excuse for such despicable slander. Devlin's a weasel. I should have finished him off then, when I had the chance.'

Mark felt a tightening in his gut and his back teeth clenched together, making his jaw ache. 'I'm glad you told me,' he said with steely quiet. 'Now go…do what you must to make your apologies to your family.' Without another word he set the curricle in motion. As he pelted through the streets towards Belgrave Crescent, one thought tormented his mind. Was it slander, or had the Viscount and Emily been lovers when they were engaged?

A bittersweet memory niggled at Mark's consciousness, made him fear the truth was the answer he didn't want. Emily had ended their first kiss too soon and, in frustration, he had made a crass remark. His attempt at conciliation had been rebuffed and she had refused to elaborate on her reasons for rejecting a compliment on her innocence. Now, with wounding insight, Mark suspected he knew what she meant by it. Once she had been Devlin's mistress as well as his betrothed. Perhaps the Viscount thought he was entitled to that intimacy again… whether she was willing or not.

'Arrange for fresh horses to be brought round. At once!'

Geoffrey Lomax gazed at his master's broad back as he strode the hallway, then took the stairs two at a time. Snapping from his daze at being on the receiving end of such uncharacteristic churlishness from Mr Hunter, the butler sprang to do his bidding.

Within minutes Mark was again in the lobby, the weight of razor-edged steel in one pocket of his greatcoat balanced by a duck's foot pistol in the other. He was not a violent man, and hoped the weapons would remain unused, but he accepted he must be prepared for any eventuality.

If Devlin were not at home this evening, Riley's slum would be his next port of call. Mark suspected that a fight would erupt if Riley's two henchmen were about. A brawl, even with odds stacked against him, would not usually bother him. Without vanity he accepted his notoriety as one of Gentleman Jackson's finest. But he did not want his mettle tested. He wanted to be fit and able to protect Emily if the need arose.

Aware that his grim-faced master was on his way out without another word passing between them, Lomax hopped to intercept him. 'Umm… there was a caller in your absence, sir. I promised to give you the lady's note as soon as you returned.'

Mark halted at once and frowned fiercely at Lomax. 'A woman came here to see me?'

'Miss Beaumont was her name, and she seemed upset to have missed you. She left a note,' Lomax concisely informed his master.

'Give it to me at once,' Mark demanded hoarsely, a hand already outstretched to receive it.

Lomax hurried to the console table and gazed in vain. He crouched on spindly legs to see if the note had dropped to the floor. He scanned an arc of marble in case it had gone further adrift.

Mark walked towards him, his expression thunderous.

'I cannot understand it, sir. I put it here. I know I did.'

'Has another servant moved it?'

'They wouldn't dare…nobody has been near nor by except…'

'Except?' Mark prompted with dangerous impatience.

A grimace of disbelief distorted the butler's features, for what he suspected, yet hesitated to mention, was outlandish…perhaps calumnious. 'Mrs Emerson called, a few minutes after Miss Beaumont left. Mrs Emerson did study her reflection in this mirror, but she said not to mention her visit, so of course I would not have done so…'

Before the servant had concluded his explanation Mark loosed a terse dismissal and strode to the door, his lips a thin white line on clenched teeth.

The note reposed on polished mahogany amid crystal perfume bottles and chased silver boxes. Barbara was seated on her little velvet boudoir chair, her dark eyes resting on the tantalising white rectangle.

Abruptly she picked it up. Her pale fingers slipped to the sealing wax, then withdrew. Irritably she tapped the paper against a thumbnail as she strove for the courage to open it. If Mark ever discovered what she had done there would be no adequate explanation for such outrageous impertinence. But now that she had stolen the note, it seemed silly to simply imagine what it might contain. Holding it to the window, or to candlelight, had elicited not a hint of what message was concealed within. With a gulped breath, and a burst of activity, Barbara tore at the wax, quickly unfolded the parchment and scanned the single paragraph.

Riley has discovered Tarquin's whereabouts, and that he is ill, and wants to see me. Riley will not disclose the exact location other than to say it is on the outskirts of town. It cannot be too distant as he promises we will return before dusk. I do not completely trust him, yet don't know what he might gain from such a lie. So I shall go with him, and do my best to persuade Tarquin that he must return to face the music. I trust we will return safely together and that you might continue to give your support and counsel to Tarquin. I wish I had found you at home to tell you all this...

Barbara frowned and read it again, then, with a

little oath, tossed it aside. It had not been worth the effort at all! She had hoped—or rather dreaded—that she had intercepted a love letter, or one that informed Mark that he'd impregnated the little trollop. But what had she got? Just drivel concerning Emily's gadabout brother and a fellow called Riley who knew where the wastrel was to be found. What cared she for any of that?

Perhaps she had been too hasty in thinking Mark and Emily were in love. Barbara picked over the words more carefully, looking for hidden meaning. Emily might have written of her regrets at not finding Mark at home, but there was no hint of passion in her prose.

A sound of pattering feet made Barbara swivel on her chair. Her maid appeared in the doorway, her small chest heaving as though she had sprinted up the stairs. 'The *monsieur* is here, *madame*, but I said he must wait below, for he looks so very angry…' The French girl shivered into silence as she sensed Mark's presence behind her.

'You may leave us, Claudine,' Barbara said, but her voice sounded shrill, and her unsteady fingers swiftly slid back and forth behind her to try to conceal the parchment with boxes and bottles.

Her fluttering fingers and flustered demeanour made a purely cynical smile touch Mark's mouth.

Barbara gained her feet in a sinuous movement and swayed towards him, arresting his progress towards the dressing table. 'This is a most pleasant surprise,' she murmured huskily and went on tiptoe with her face tilted as though to kiss him.

Mark caught the twin white limbs that would have snaked about his neck. Keeping a firm grip on her wrists, he pulled her with him towards the dressing table. A perfume pot crashed to its side, filling the air with musky scent, as he carelessly cleared the note of obstacles. But for a tic close to his mouth, Mark's face remained impassive as he read Emily's cry for help.

'I…I came to see you earlier,' Barbara started in a rush, disturbed by his peculiar stillness. 'You were out. When I said I might soon chance upon you in Hyde Park, Lomax gave me the letter to take to you…' Her words faded away to awkward silence, but it was not her fluent lie unsettling her as much as the vivid blue eyes boring coldly into her.

'Is that so?' Mark asked in a voice of silky steel. 'For the moment we will ignore the poor likelihood of any such meeting. What excuse have you for opening a letter addressed to me?'

Barbara's cheeks bloomed beneath his contempt. 'It might have been a pressing matter,' she breathed, in a burst of inspiration. 'Indeed, I deemed it to be of a vital nature, for your butler to want it so quickly delivered,' she smoothly reasoned with a winning smile. 'When I could not see you in the Park I thought I ought to open it and find out if that were so, in case I should search for you elsewhere.'

Mark grunted a mirthless laugh and extricated his hand from fingers that had crept to erotically fondle his palm. 'You're a mischief-maker, Barbara, amongst other things.' He strode away from her and was again at the door when he added, 'It's a pity it has come to this between us. I've no time now to say more, but I think you already suspect how I feel. In any case, know this: I despise liars and thieves.'

As Mark leaped from his curricle outside the Beaumonts' home, Tarquin hurtled down the steps as though he had been waiting for his friend to hove into view.

'Thank God you're back! Emily is not at home and hasn't been seen since early this afternoon,' Tarquin gabbled, his brows drawn tight together in consternation.

Mark felt a stab of anguish. It was the news he had expected, yet dreaded to hear, from one of the Beaumonts.

'My parents are not yet too concerned—they think she is probably gone off with her friend Sarah Harper. They often spend many hours together. Let's see if she is at Sarah's. It's not far…'

'She isn't there,' Mark bleakly dashed Tarquin's hopes whilst raking fingers through his dark hair. Abruptly he pulled from a pocket Emily's note and thrust it at Tarquin.

Tarquin moved to stand beneath the pale light of a gas lamp to scan it. 'Damnation! Jenny was right! He's used the very trick she mentioned. We're too late. Devlin's got her.' This last was uttered in a voice that vibrated with horrified disbelief.

'But where? Where has he got her?' Mark clipped out in a tone that hinted at desperation. He strove to stay calm. The boundary of his control was crumbling. But to succumb to rage would defeat reason. And then he would never help Emily. Her note was a tangible proof of her trust in him. In the lines of her composition he had sensed her heartfelt plea that he must come to her rescue if it transpired that Riley was up to no good. Mark tipped back his head and aimed a string of foul curses at the emerging stars. If only he had been at home when she called. But he had been in Enfield, evicting her brother from the hunting lodge. He squeezed shut his eyes, but the hideous images of Emily's torment would not quit his mind.

'Riley will have gone to ground,' he reasoned hoarsely. 'He will have suspected that Emily would not go with him without leaving a message of sorts with someone she trusted. He is wily enough to know that person would come looking for him when Emily did not return.' Mark paced to and fro, his hands plunged deep into his pockets, his face a study of savage concentration. 'Devlin will have arranged that Emily be taken to an isolated spot. Without Riley leading us there, it will be impossible to find it.'

'Jenny will have a few ideas where Riley hides out.' Tarquin's face grew animated. 'We can go and beat out of him where he has taken Emily.' Tarquin's bright expression crumpled and he aimed a grimace at the Beaumont residence. 'I've deflected my parents' questions so far with lame excuses. My father is too disgusted with me to stay in my company for long.' He paused. 'But Mother is a constant shadow. I had a devil of a job escaping just now. She attempted to drag me back by my coat-tails when I said I was off out with you.' He shook his head in despair as he dwelled on their likely reaction to knowing of their daughter's jeopardy. 'We must bring Emily back, whatever that bastard has done to her. If she is sullied, we must make sure that we are the only ones who know of it.'

'It won't come to that!' Mark gritted out and turned on Tarquin eyes that resembled ebony slits. 'We must make sure it doesn't come to that.'

Tarquin quickly nodded, keen to pacify his friend. He had known for a while that Mark was soft on Emily. His friend was sensibly attempting to direct his energy into solving the riddle of Emily's whereabouts. But until they had an inkling of where that might be they were powerless to save her, and Mark's simmering frustration was close to erupting in violence.

'If we manage to snatch Emily from his clutches, Devlin might threaten to spread gossip from spite,' Mark said. 'He knows it is Emily who will suffer most from a scandal.'

'I'll cut out his tongue if he does that!' Tarquin said. 'After that, I'll take his black heart.'

'You need to keep a cool head until Emily is safe.' Within a moment he had added on an insightful sigh, 'We both do…'

As though fearing Mark might refuse his company, Tarquin sprang aboard the curricle and settled firmly into the seat. 'There's no time to lose. Let's go and find Jenny. I'll wager she's privy to Riley's hidey-holes.' He cast a worried look homeward and noticed his mother peering at him between the curtains. 'My father will kill me if Emily is harmed!' he groaned.

'He won't. I will,' Mark vowed with perilous quiet before he joined Tarquin on the seat.

had Whitley found a worthwhile opponent here without his novice hesitation and self-mockery?

... 'I believe will withstand what is to come.'

The monk began to recite with a dry chant ...

Chapter Thirteen

'You have planned this quite meticulously.' Emily raised her goblet and let ruby wine just moisten her lips. She had no intention of allowing Nicholas to get her tipsy. But there might be an advantage in fostering his mellow humour and letting him think she was tolerant of his company and his hospitality. The less he thought she was inclined to escape the more likely she was to successfully do so.

The initial shock of having been kidnapped had lessened and Emily had come to the conclusion that expending energy on angry complaints would be foolish. Better, surely, to employ the same craftiness that had been used against her.

She guessed she had now been in captivity for some hours although she had no idea of the exact time. It seemed the only people at the house were the manservant who had opened the door, and a young maid who had shown her to a chamber to make ready to dine.

Despite her fright and simmering anger, Emily had been grateful for the sanctuary it provided. She had been tired and dusty after her headlong trip with Riley and felt unprepared to pit her wits immediately against her captor.

The chamber had been warm and steaming scented washing water had helped to soothe her fraught senses. Emily had dismissed the maid despite the girl's insistence that she must press her crumpled dress and style her hair. Emily had had no intention of allowing herself to be primped for the benefit of the scheming lecher waiting for her below. She had also wanted the maid gone from the room in order to investigate possible escape routes. But a swift inspection had revealed that every window was sealed and the door had been locked from outside. That discovery had set Emily's pulse racing alarmingly. In a moment desolation had overwhelmed her and brought scalding tears to sting her weary eyes.

From the moment Riley had departed, leaving her alone with the Viscount and his minions, she had not given up hope that she might soon manage to flee. But it seemed that Nicholas had schooled his servants well. Both his butler and his maidservant had cooperated in her incarceration.

By the time the maid had returned Emily had curbed the craven instinct to wail and plead for liberation and was more composed. With the girl's encouragement she had freshened herself with the lavender-water and untangled the knots from her blonde tresses well enough to tease them into a plain chignon. Her pride in her appearance had been solely for her own benefit. She had resolved not to appear before Nicholas looking a wreck lest he believed he had managed to cow her. She would not snivel, nor would she outwardly quake even if her insides felt like jelly. She would certainly never willingly do his bidding. Once she had believed he cherished her, and had proved she trusted him by gifting him her body. Now she would fight him with her last breath rather than tolerate even a kiss from him.

As she had followed the girl down the wide carpeted stairway, Emily had been oblivious to her plush surroundings. Her thoughts had been with her parents. She had drawn comfort from the recollection that they had an invitation for this evening. If they returned late from the opera they might retire without ever knowing their daughter's bed was empty. There was yet time to avert their heart-ache…and a scandal. But she must get home, and to do that she must pray that Mark came to her rescue in time.

She would remain optimistic, she vowed beneath her breath, her fingers stressfully tightening in her lap. By now Mark would have her note and be immediately suspicious as to Riley's motives for taking her out of town. He would go to Callison Crescent and, without alerting her parents to her jeopardy, discover she had not returned home. Then he would search for Riley and interrogate the duplicitous pimp until he admitted he had tricked her into going with him, and revealed her whereabouts.

Having thus boosted her morale, she resented the small inner voice that would rob her of such sweet confidence. *But what if Mark cannot find Riley?* it whispered. Perhaps he might be injured in the pursuit of the villain. And plainly there was a chance he might not yet have returned home to take delivery of her note. He was a leading light of polite society with family, friends and a mistress to occupy his time. He might not return to his own home or bed at all tonight…

Emily forgot her rule to be abstemious. She took

a spontaneous gulp from her wine to steady her pounding heart. If only Mark had been at home when she called! Abruptly she deposited the glass on the table, fearing it might shatter in her bone-white clutch. She fought down the panic tightening her chest and gulped in a steadying breath.

A calculating look flew from under her lashes at the man seated opposite her. To keep at bay his advances, she must engage him in conversation. Eventually she might prick his conscience, and persuade him to go home to his wife.

'You have been deep in thought, my love. Have you concocted a plot to escape?' Nicholas's torrid gaze swept over her, lingering where the rapidity of her breathing was straining the buttons on her bodice.

Emily felt her cheeks tingle; he was close to reading her mind. 'Escape?' She gurgled a laugh and made a dismissive gesture. 'Do you expect I might resort to running around aimlessly in the cold and dark?' Her tone was scornful, yet in truth she would most definitely choose the night, and the unknown countryside, over him.

'Is this house yours or have you acquired it simply as a theatre for seduction?' She inwardly praised herself for sounding so calm when it was hard to keep her teeth from chattering. Her sleek fair head turned this way and that as she studied the stylish furnishings bathed in an ambience from logs burning in the grate. 'It is a fine stage. Should I be flattered that I merit such lavish treatment?'

Devlin gave a throaty chuckle. 'I am pleased to know that you are still my proud, intrepid Emily. No tears…no tantrums…you know deep in your heart, my love, that we are destined to be together, do you not?'

'You have not answered my question, Nicholas,' Emily scolded breathily.

'The property was one of many that came to me on marriage as part of my wife's dowry. But what matter its origins? I'm glad you like it—we shall make regular use of it. It shall be our special place to meet. Perhaps—if you greatly please me—I might eventually make it yours.'

'How kind… But I'm not sure that I like it that much,' Emily returned acidly. 'And I doubt your wife would appreciate the use to which you put her property.'

'It is no longer her property and we will not speak of her again.'

'Why ever not?' Emily demanded pithily. The longer they conversed about his duty to his family, the more confident Emily became that he might relent. 'Would you deny your wife's existence? Or that of your unborn child?'

Nicholas forcefully thrust away his plate, making Emily start and drop her fork. It seemed she had softened him not one jot.

'I suspect you are about to moralise and we both know you are hardly a lady fit to do so.'

'And you are hardly a gentleman to have reminded me,' Emily returned. She had expected a reference would be made to their one night of passion and had steeled herself to parry it. Yet she could feel tingling in her face and queasiness in her belly from the shame of it. Her brazen riposte remained blocked in her dry throat.

'I am not complaining about your passionate nature, my dear, as I'm sure you know.' Nicholas gave a lascivious chuckle as he noticed the roses in her cheeks spread to her throat.

'I thought I loved you, Nicholas, and it ill behoves you to mock my sincere emotion. Had I not been so young, and so very naïve, I would have understood that, for you, I was just sport. When I lay with you, I truly believed we soon would be man and wife.'

'And I truly regret it could not be,' Nicholas drawled. 'Alas, you tempted me with your body, my dear, but had no such desirable dowry.' He smiled wryly. 'I must say that, for just a few thousand more, I might have forgone an heiress…'

'I doubt it,' Emily snapped. His flippancy had fired her anger to such a degree her trepidation was evaporating.

'I do too,' he conceded with an impenitent smile. 'A woman with thirty thousand, and a property portfolio of the same value, has undeniable allure for a man with pockets to let.'

'You tricked me with lies and promises. You had no intention of marrying me, did you?' Emily accused.

Nicholas shrugged and spread his hands in a show of insolent apology.

'Our betrothal was a sham. You proposed simply so you might seduce me.'

Nicholas sighed in irritation and shoved himself back in his chair. 'Do not make me out the heartless villain.' He eyed her through lowered lashes. 'You were ripe for love, innocent yet wanton, and took little persuading that night.'

Emily's soft lips parted in shock and indignation at such brutal honesty. But then she ought to know by now that Nicholas was careless of wounding her ego. A small corner of her mind acknowledged too that, young or not when engaged, she had been a credulous fool to be so totally blind to his true character. The only consolation was in knowing that she had not been the only one taken in by his lies. He had duped her parents too with his smooth talk of love and honour.

'You will find I am very different now, Nicholas,' Emily said coldly. 'I have no liking for you, let alone any stronger feelings…'

'Enough!' Nicholas snapped before Emily could amplify her disgust. 'I would far sooner treat you gently, Emily… share the pleasure with you.'

'You are a fool if you think you can get away with this,' Emily pointed out quite levelly although her moist palms were quivering in her lap. 'How do you intend to explain away having kidnapped and forced your attentions on a gentlewoman? By now my parents will be worried for my safety. The authorities will have been notified. You will be arrested once the truth is out.'

Nicholas snorted an unconcerned laugh. 'And who will tell the truth? You? Your parents? The last thing any of you want is for our affair—now or in the past—to be common knowledge. Your reputation would be irrevocably lost and your family would share in your shame.' The wine goblet performed a balletic twirl between his fingers. 'You were willing once; who would not believe you were willing again?' He smiled, almost sympathetically. 'You would not lie under oath, Emily, and deny we were lovers. You must accept that it is meant to be. Fate and your brother's folly have happily reunited us.'

'Which house?' Mark's voice was eerily soft as he addressed Jenny, but his eyes glittered hard and bright as ebony stars. A scouting look assessed the vicinity. In the meagre light he could just see that Jenny had directed him to the heart of a London slum. Stumpy terraces wobbled like rows of rotten teeth on lanes that yawned in four directions.

Jenny was wedged between the two men in the curricle. She nodded at a property that looked slightly less dilapidated than its neighbours. A weak lamp was burning in the ground-floor window. 'I reckon he might be in there gaming. When he's flush he likes to play dice for big stakes. I came here once before with him.' She swallowed and her wide dark eyes swung between the two men. 'You both best be careful. There are coves who hang around with him who'd crack your skulls open soon as look at you.'

'Can't Riley fight his own battles?' Tarquin scoffed, seemingly unperturbed by the idea of a brawl.

Jenny's top lip curled. 'He's a coward who saves his beatings for the girls who work for him. He got that broken nose off his pa for backchat when he was a youngster.'

Tarquin's lips twitched at the anecdote then, disengaging his elbow from Jenny's fearful grip, and with a fierce instruction to her to sit tight till he returned, he followed Mark towards the building.

'If I jump, you're in big trouble.'

'So are you,' Mark returned without bothering to take a look at the man trussed beside him.

Riley wriggled in his bonds and flung himself back against the squabs. 'Anything happens to me, you'll never find her.'

'And if I don't find her…a great many things *will* happen to you. That's a promise,' Mark said with tranquil menace. His cool demeanour admirably concealed that his anguish was mounting by the minute.

He had long known Devlin for a debauchee, but never before had he believed him capable of such dastardly behaviour. In abducting Emily he had proved himself to be a ruthless criminal too. But how far would he go to assuage his lust? Would he resort to physical violence if Emily resisted his attempt to charm her into bed? Would he ply her with drink and rape her helpless, comatose body? Emily was Devlin's captive, at his mercy for him to do with her what he would! Mark felt the agony writhe again deep in his gut as vile images of Emily's torment rotated in his brain.

He loved Emily Beaumont and had wanted to ask her to marry him. Had she been his betrothed she would have been protected by his name. Devlin would not have dared corner her to demand a kiss, let alone more. How would he ever forgive himself if she were harmed? A groaning oath tore from between his lips and he urged the horses to a faster pace. He must find her and there was only one man who could lead him to her. He'd use verbal persuasion to start, but if that didn't work he'd do whatever was necessary. God only knew the villain beside him deserved a beating for what he'd done to Jenny, let alone his part in this evil plan.

Abruptly he turned his head and a gaze so replete with loathing was levelled at his reluctant passenger that Riley shrank back into the corner of the vehicle. 'You're in deep trouble,' he gritted through his teeth. 'The sensible course of action would be for you to assist in righting the wrong you've done to Miss Beaumont. In a judge's eyes, it might redeem you slightly and lessen the severity of his sentence.'

'I'll swing anyhow if Jenny croaks.'

Mark's face tautened into bleak lines at the reminder of the disturbance he'd left behind in town.

Jenny had not taken Tarquin's advice and stayed in the curricle. Instead she had slipped inside—probably to assist and keep Tarquin from harm—when a fight erupted. Riley had had his henchmen with him and, whilst Mark and Tarquin were battling with them, Mickey Riley had noticed his nemesis hovering in the corridor. Realising that Jenny had betrayed him, the ruffian had battered her savagely to the ground. Jenny was rendered unconscious before Tarquin or Mark realised she was in the house.

Within minutes Mark had left Tarquin tending to his limp, bleeding wife and set off towards the Surrey border with Riley cursing and squirming beside him. Now that his bruisers were unable to save him Riley had quietened, but Mark knew that his foxy brain was constantly calculating methods of escape.

'If you want to jump, go ahead,' Mark snarled. 'There's a good chance it won't kill you…not straight away, anyhow. The sight of your broken limbs won't bother me. As long as you're able to talk, that's good enough.'

Riley kicked out in frustration at the side of the vehicle, then slouched into the seat with a sullen scowl on his face.

Mark reined back as they approached a cross-roads. 'Which way?'

Riley remained uncommunicative. When Mark slid along the seat towards him and repeated his question in a voice of silky steel, the villain jerked his head to the right.

Immediately Mark snatched up the reins, whipped leather over the backs of the horses, and they sped off again into the night.

The meal was coming to an end and with it Emily's capacity for conversation. She felt exhausted and fearful. Nicholas would feel entitled to strike now he had acted the gallant and wined and dined her. She slipped her unsteady fingers to the dinner knife she had secreted in the folds of her skirts. She hoped she would not need to utilise it, but she had no intention of quietly going upstairs with him!

Oh, where was Mark? Why had he not come to her rescue? Once she had shunned his touch; what would she not give now to rest within his powerful embrace?

Emily dropped the spoon with which she had idly been stirring her syllabub and jumped to her feet. While she had been deep in wistful reverie Nicholas had made his move. He had gained half the length of the table, and his expression was unmistakably predatory. Before she could properly extricate herself from her chair to flee, he was trapping her against it.

With a low chuckle he twisted the dinner knife from her fist, for he had anticipated her defensive tactics. Mockingly he clucked disapproval as he dropped the silver on to mahogany. His hard fingers were tight as manacles on her wrists as he brought his face closer to hers.

Emily's back bowed as she tried to avoid his lips travelling on her throat. His murmured endearments steamed on her skin and then his mouth pounced, forcing apart her lips, so his tongue could thrust within.

Emily twisted in his grasp, but his unpleasant laugh met her futile attempts to free herself. He was enjoying curbing her struggles, she realised, and she would not knowingly give him pleasure. Abruptly she became still, allowed him to nuzzle at her neck whilst her averted eyes darted to what lay on the table that might serve as a weapon. Her flitting glance returned to the grand silver candelabra. It was quite close and its weight would do far more damage than the dainty porcelain crockery within easy reach. The knife he'd taken from her had skidded some distance on the polished surface, but a fork was tantalisingly near to the fingers she had splayed on the table edge for support.

Swallowing her revulsion at the Viscount's fingers exploring her bodice fastenings, she forced herself to relax and tolerate a kiss. Coquettishly she twisted her head away. 'Do you really regret not marrying me, Nicholas?' she gulped whilst slyly edging sideways. 'I should like to think that at least is the truth.'

'Of course it's the truth,' he growled on an impatient pant and planted his hot mouth against the rapid pulse at the base of her throat.

Emily squirmed in his grasp, loosening his hold enough to allow her to sidle a step closer to the fork, barely an inch from her outstretched fingers. 'You're not just saying it to seduce me more easily?' she wheedled.

Nicholas raised his head, gazed at her with hot amber eyes. 'I said I'd rather share the pleasure with you, Emily,' he answered huskily. 'I'm not a violent man…but I can be when I'm desperate.' He cupped her chin in a hard hand. 'I want you…I'm desperate to have you. Why are you being cruel?'

He made the complaint with such genuine perplexity in his voice that Emily could barely repress a snort of derisive amazement.

'Be kind to me, my love!' Nicholas demanded hoarsely. 'Then I shall be kind to you.' He tried to prove his point by biting against Emily's throat with less brutality.

'I'm afraid I can't, for you disgust me,' Emily gasped and, snatching up the fork from the table, used all her might to stab him in the thigh.

Nicholas yelped and tottered back, a hand massaging furiously at the wound she'd delivered.

Emily raced to grab the silver candlestick and brandished it with both hands. 'Stay away, you vile swine, or I swear I'll use this on you!' she cried.

Nicholas gave a final rub to the puncture in his flesh. 'You little bitch,' he enunciated slowly. 'You will certainly pay for that.' He twisted his mouth into a sneer. 'And if you think a candlestick will save you, you are a silly little fool.' He paced purposefully closer, making Emily retreat in time with his advance. 'You are exceeding all my expectations, my dear. Fight me if you will. I'll enjoy taming you. I should have told you that it's the chase… the victory…that I need above all else.'

Just as Emily was rallying strength to launch her missile at him, a noise made her hesitate and whip her head around. But what she saw made her realise that the interruption was a reprieve, not deliverance. The manservant was hovering on the threshold of the dining room. A neutral expression was shaping his brawny features as though it was not uncommon for him to witness a young lady about to fend off his master's advances with a flaming candelabra.

Nicholas's face was a mask of fury and a few crude curses were spat out as he strode towards the fellow.

The servant hastened to meet him, now with an intensely apologetic look on his face. Quickly he whispered a message and, in return, received a curt nod, and a muttered instruction from his master.

'It seems that Mr Riley has returned for some reason best known to himself.' Nicholas's tone was rough with irritation. 'Please excuse me just for a moment, my dear, while I impress on the dolt that he is *de trop* and very much unwelcome.' He gave her a subtle smile. 'I will not abandon you for long, I promise, but be seated again.' His former suave composure seemed to be restored. A theatrical hand flicked specks from an immaculate sleeve. 'There is no escape; my servants are utterly loyal to me. So… why not relax and finish your syllabub whilst you wait for my return?'

Nicholas had instructed his manservant to stop the pimp setting foot inside the house. He therefore strode out directly on to the canopied porch with a snapped, 'I hope you have an excellent reason for this impertinence, Riley…'

'He has,' Mark drawled as he emerged from the shadows cast by the eaves. 'He doesn't want a bullet lodged in his black heart.' The duck's foot pistol was held in a steady hand against Mickey Riley's chest. Abruptly Mark realigned the weapon so both men were in its range. 'As for you, Devlin, a bullet strategically placed elsewhere might suit.' Mark indicated with a wave of the weapon that they should go inside the house.

'Do you mind telling me what the hell this is all about?' Devlin blustered, affecting outrage. He sent Riley a purely poisonous look.

'I think you know exactly what this is about, Devlin,' Mark responded with icy calm. 'Where is Miss Beaumont?'

Devlin licked his lips. He had not for a moment anticipated that a knight in shining armour might turn up and scotch his plans to force Emily to become his mistress.

'I shall quite happily persuade you to answer,' Mark said. 'I have enough ammunition to make life very uncomfortable for you both.'

'Miss Beaumont is presently eating her dinner,

Hunter,' the Viscount uttered quickly. His mind ferreted for explanations as to what prompted this man's interference. He knew that Tarquin Beaumont and Mark Hunter were friends, but he sensed that Hunter's involvement might be due to a more personal interest in Emily. Nicholas had been aware that soppy Stephen Bond was sniffing about her, but not that a fellow of Hunter's stature was in the running for Emily's affections. It was time to mark his territory, even if in doing so he sullied Emily's reputation.

He gave Mark a conspiratorial smile. 'I think you must recall, Hunter, that the lady and I once were betrothed. Alas, it came to nought but we still are *passionately* fond of each other.' He spread his hands appealingly. 'There, I have said it. You are privy now to our secret. It is a delicate situation, but we are both men of the world. I know you would not intentionally ruin a spinster's future marriage prospects by breathing a word of this to anyone.'

'No…but you would, and give little thought to the consequences for her and her family,' Emily uttered in a gruff little voice. She had immediately followed Nicholas from the dining room. So confident was he of his servant's loyalty and vigilance that he had not bothered to lock her in. Now she moved forward, slowly at first, but her relief at seeing Mark prompted her to skip swiftly to his side.

A strong arm immediately secured her there, heavy and possessive about her quivering shoulders. The hand holding the pistol did not waver from its target.

Devlin's eyes narrowed on the couple. Emily had quite naturally curved into Mark Hunter's embrace as though she had done so before. He smiled grimly. 'Perhaps the two of you have been keeping secrets of your own—' he began, but his insinuation was immediately curtailed by Mark's voice.

'I know you won't object if we are immediately on our way.' Mark swung a look between the two men and his lip curled slightly. 'I imagine the two of you have scores to settle.' Keeping the gun steady on them, he led Emily towards the door.

'You must think you're pretty clever, to get the better of me,' Devlin gritted in furious frustration as he watched Emily slipping from his grasp.

'No…not really,' Mark answered. 'What I do think is that you're pretty stupid to think you'd get away with such an outrage.' Mark suddenly raised the pistol and fired a shot at the brightly flickering chandelier. The chain was severed and crystal and brass crashed to the floor, plunging the hallway into blackness. Swiftly Mark turned and, with Emily fast in his embrace, urged her out into the night.

Chapter Fourteen

'I knew you'd come to rescue me.'

'And are you glad I did?'

Emily sent her saviour a somewhat startled look. She had intended her vibrant declaration to convey her praise and gratitude, yet Mark's response had sounded cynical. 'Could you not tell how pleased… how relieved I was to see you?' she demanded, rather piqued.

'Given the circumstances it would have been ill advised to look disappointed. You might once have been betrothed to your kidnapper, nevertheless you have your reputation to consider.'

'What do you mean by that?' Emily breathed fiercely. She had been feeling quite enervated by the day's chaotic events, but now her temper was stirring, sparking vitality into her. 'Do you think I was pleased to find the Viscount had plotted to abduct me?'

'I believe that once you would have been pleased to be the Viscount's wife.'

Emily felt the full force of his trenchant blue gaze. Her chin went up, but her heart plummeted. Whilst she had been in captivity, Mark had soared so high in her estimation that she feared she might be coming to like him very much indeed. He had been her hero, the man on whom she had pinned all her hopes. She'd trusted he would bring everything right and, up until a few moments ago, he'd lived up to every expectation. In fact, so beguiled by him had she become, she had acknowledged that he stirred her heart…and body…in a way that no man had, even Nicholas…

Now he had ruined it all. He had just forced her to recall that recently she had been sure she didn't like him. Suddenly she felt quite depressed…quite sad.

'It's true Nicholas and I were betrothed many years ago,' Emily eventually said. 'He now has a wife. I hope you are not hinting I might welcome the attentions of a married man.'

'And if he were not married?'

'It would make no difference,' Emily returned immediately.

'Devlin mentioned you were still *passionately* fond of one another.'

'Well, he had no right to say any such thing! It is a lie!' Emily choked. 'I loathe him, and I don't believe he likes me much either. If he had any kind of regard for me, he would not have wanted to treat me so abominably. Not that any of it is your business.' Emily paused after that outburst, fiddled with her cuffs. 'I have satisfied your inquisitiveness simply because you have gone out of your way to assist me today.' Her voice was husky with emotion and spontaneous tears shone in her eyes. A hand sprang to her face to irritably dash the wet away.

As they had thundered towards London Mark had enquired if she were warm enough, if she wanted to make an early stop. Beneath his courteous consideration for her comfort Emily had sensed that he was in a brooding mood. She had anticipated an early interrogation, even a scolding for having put herself in jeopardy by going off alone with Riley. What she had not expected was this odd atmosphere that had erected a barrier between them. On the journey, when her attempts at conversation received a monosyllable in reply, she'd lapsed into quiet. She had at first imagined Mark was preoccupied with putting distance between the curricle and possible pursuers.

Emily now suspected the space he'd wanted to maintain was between them.

Since they had joined forces to solve the mystery of Tarquin's disappearance, she had grown accustomed to those blue eyes smouldering at her in humour or desire. Now he was different; his attitude was unerringly polite but aloof. And she didn't like it. She wanted soothing words and strong arms comforting her. She wanted his approval and his affection…

'I'm sorry, Emily, I didn't mean to upset you.' Mark pinched at strain between his brows, feeling churlish in the extreme at having let suspicion conquer courtesy. Since he had discovered Emily had been tricked into going with Riley, and for what vile purpose, he had been frantic with worry for her safety. Now, instead of cherishing the gift of her presence, and her safe deliverance, he was acting like a jealous buffoon.

Emily had endured more than enough already today, yet he had just added to her troubles. His hand slid to enclose quivering white fingers. 'I had no right to say any of that, or pry into your past. Forgive me…?'

When Emily remained silent, Mark sat back in his chair with a heavy sigh. 'For hours I've been dreading what your captor might do to you, Emily.' His admission was quiet, almost diffident. 'Devlin tried to make light of it all. He hinted you were a willing participant and had a secret life as his mistress…it maddened me.' He passed a hand roughly over his face. 'I'm a fool, I know, to suspect one word that bastard uttered might be the truth.'

Feeling reassured by the explanation for his bad mood, Emily twisted her wrist beneath his to clasp his palm. 'I was so very glad you came for me, Mark,' Emily stressed softly. 'It was only the thought that soon you would burst in to rescue me that kept my spirits up.' Her small fingers tightened reflexively about his as a wave of relief shuddered through her. 'I prayed you would get my note in time and find clues to where Riley had taken me. Had I lost hope and trust in you, I doubt I would have found the strength to resist.' Her voice trembled into silence and she stifled a sob with her knuckles. 'I stabbed Nicholas in the leg with a fork to get free and was about to throw a candelabra at him when you turned up.'

Mark chuckled softly, raised her fingers to his lips and tenderly saluted them. 'Devlin was never a match for you.'

The inflection in Mark's voice made Emily sure he was not simply referring to her plucky attack on Devlin.

Gently, reluctantly, Mark disengaged his hand from fingers that felt temptingly sensual. He used it to grab his glass and take a swallow of brandy. 'Drink your wine before it cools. It will revive you. We still have many miles to travel.' He pushed her hot toddy closer to her on the table.

Emily rewarded him with a smile and gratefully toasted her cool palms on the steaming cup. Quickly she took a glance about at her cosy surroundings.

It had been impossible to safely travel on without allowing the horses to be rested and watered. They had broken their journey at this wayside inn on the Guildford Road. The saloon bar of the Rose and Crown had been crowded with boisterous locals so Mark had taken a private room for them. The landlord—a jovial fellow with a patch over one eye that lent him an incongruously piratical air so far inland—had shown them to the back parlour of the establishment. Whilst leading the way through the narrow corridors, he had apologised profusely that they could not have the best parlour, but that, he explained, had been taken earlier by a family on their way to Guildford. The other he had available was very nice, he'd assured them, and so it proved to be. It was small, but quite clean and tidy and adequately furnished. Once ensconced in wing chairs positioned on either side of the glowing grate, Mark had assured her they would be back on the road within an hour and in Mayfair before midnight.

In truth, Emily had been grateful for the stop. Since they'd set out back to London at breakneck speed there had been no proper opportunity for much conversation to pass between them. After their recent fraught exchange, Emily wasn't sure whether she would rather maintain this amicable quiet than have the answers to the pressing questions rotating in her mind. It seemed talking invariably led to bickering. But she knew they must talk, and at great length, for there was so much she needed to know.

What news was there of Tarquin? What would happen to Riley, and to Viscount Devlin? Mark had said Nicholas would pay and so he should. Such despicable behaviour deserved punishment. But a scandal? Please, no! Her parents did not deserve to be embarrassed by their foolish daughter as well as their wayward son.

Mark watched flitting emotions etch strain on Emily's heart-shaped countenance. Wisps of fair hair had escaped from the knot at the back of her head to embellish skin made luminous by misty night air. Her eyes were languid with sleepiness, the lids low.

Mark needed answers to those questions that still pitilessly tortured him. The Viscount had schemed to trap Emily today, and she was genuinely angry over it. But had she once willingly been Devlin's mistress? If so, would he have eventually again coaxed her into consenting to sleep with him?

Mark took a swig from his brandy, aware that he felt ashamed of the quickening in his loins. She looked desirable despite her ordeal, too beautifully vulnerable to be alone with a man who wanted her as much as he did. Despite their differences, he knew she trusted him, felt safe with him, yet he could not banish the lustful thoughts pricking his mind.

He suspected she was not as innocent as a genteel spinster ought to be. But how experienced was she? Had Devlin taken her maidenhead, or had his devilish plot been devised so he might finish what he'd started years ago?

Mark rose abruptly and strolled to the window. He struck a broad hand on the frame and looked into the blackness, his thoughts as hot as his loins. If he were to kiss her…and she were to melt against him as she had done before…what harm in that? They were miles from home and prying eyes, and if she were knowing and compliant…there were rooms upstairs…

'Are you hungry? Would you like something to eat?' Mark asked abruptly. He shoved back from the window and paced to and fro to ease his rigid muscles.

'I'm not hungry at all. I ate dinner with Nicholas…' Emily glimpsed an immediate fierce light in Mark's eyes at another mention of the Viscount. Quickly she added, 'At first I thought it best to humour him as much as possible and accept his hospitality, while I waited for you.' Inclining her blonde head, she brought her cup close to her lips and took a sip from it. She was obliquely aware of Mark's jerky movement as he snatched up the decanter and refilled his glass.

'Very wise…' he eventually said with barely a hint of irony. His empty glass was replaced abruptly on the table.

'Are you still angry with me?' Emily asked quietly. She gave him a sweet, tentative smile. 'I know I have put you to a lot of trouble. I know it was rash to go with Riley. Actually, it was a stupid risk; I know it now I have had time to think sensibly on it. But I honestly thought Tarquin might be in peril.' She traced the rim of her cup with a slender finger, watching the movement as she said, 'I was terrified my brother might die all alone…cold and hungry.'

Her soft lower lip was nipped between worrying teeth. 'I didn't know what to do; that was why I came to try to find you at your home.' She sighed and shook her head. 'I hoped so much that you would be there to counsel me.' She finished what was left of her mulled wine, then made a rueful admission. 'That's not quite true. I didn't want your advice; I wanted you to take away the burden of it all and deal with it for me.'

'And I would have done that, I swear, Emily,' Mark vowed huskily. 'I'm not angry with you. But I am angry with Devlin and Riley, and with your dolt of a brother who brought about this fiasco. I'm angry with myself too.'

Emily would have interrupted at that point, but Mark gestured for her silence. 'Let's not speak of any of it again tonight.' A long finger moved on her cheek, teasing back a stray curl that spiralled close to her mouth. 'You're safe and that's the most important thing.' He tilted up her face so she must look at him. 'You're tired and overwrought, as is natural considering what you have been through. And if that were not enough to get you immediately back to Callison Crescent, there is your family to think about. We must get you home, and hope you have not been missed.' A frown corrugated his brow beneath a fall of dark hair. 'Heaven only knows what excuse will satisfy your parents if they have noticed your absence.' Mark gently urged Emily to her feet and, fetching her cloak, courteously placed it about her shoulders. 'If you are ready, it's high time we set again on the road.'

'Mr Hunter?'

Mark halted immediately on hearing his name barked in a cultured female voice. He turned his head. What he saw caused him enough dismay to make him swear beneath his breath, although his expression altered not one iota.

Emily was positioned slightly in front of Mark, and her slender frame had tensed statue-still for she, too, had recognized those haughty tones. Even before Mark's low curse reached her ears she knew she was once more that day in awful trouble. Her stomach lurched, and she pressed a hand against the wall to help support her on legs that felt boneless.

'I thought I recognised you, sir.' Mrs Violet Pearson emerged fully from the doorway of the Rose and Crown's best parlour. She pulled her shawl tight about her scrawny arms to ward off the chill. But her inquisitiveness had been roused far too much for her to yet go back inside and seek the warmth of the blazing logs.

When her son, Bertie, had gone upstairs to bed in a sulk, he had not properly closed the door behind him. Violet had cast a purposeful look at Mr Pearson, but he had contrived to nod off in the chair at that precise moment. Violet had thus stomped to perform the office herself rather than tolerate the draught. Just for the once she was glad that her husband and son could be lazy and inconsiderate for, as she put a hand to wood to push the door shut, she had spied something very interesting indeed in the corridor.

A lady and gentleman, glimpsed through the aperture, had seemed familiar to her. For the fleeting moment she had them in her sights Violet had been instantly put in mind of another kind of familiarity: the kind shared by people in love. Not that Violet had experience of such sweet intimacy with Mr Pearson, but she conversely relished the bitterness the lack provoked.

Violet was sure she could scent a rat…or rather a scandal, for although she had not got a good view of the young woman with Mr. Hunter, she had got a peep at golden hair curling beneath a bonnet. She also recalled seeing a classic profile and an enviably curvaceous figure. Few women could boast such remarkable attractions, and grace of movement. Naturally, she would never let on to the chit, or her mother, that she thought her pretty. So *could* it be Miss Emily Beaumont?

Violet knew that Mark Hunter and Tarquin Beaumont were chums, so there was a connection of sorts between Emily and Mark. But it seemed remarkably odd that the two of them might be at an inn, halfway to Guildford, at ten of the clock at night. Perhaps Miss Beaumont was with a relation who was elsewhere in the building…or perhaps she was not…

Violet's riotous imaginings turned her mind feverish and her face florid. Suddenly she jerked to her senses as she became aware that Mark Hunter was almost at the door, and on the point of exiting the building now he had returned her a nod and a muttered greeting.

Violet sought swiftly to detain him. 'Fancy bumping into you here, sir,' she called shrilly, speeding in his wake. 'Are you going, as we are, to the Festival in Guildford? Last year it was a delight; the orchestra and the singing divine…'

'No, ma'am,' Mark replied with a hint of irritation clipping his tone. 'I'm travelling in the opposite direction towards London.'

Violet Pearson was not so easily put off by a dark look and a curt response. She sidled the corridor wall, her head leading the way as she tried to get a better look at the dainty female partially obliterated by Mark's large frame. Violet's tongue flicked excitedly to her lips; she was very aware that the fellow was deliberately trying to shield his companion from view. A glitter brightened her eyes. Would she be returning to town with a juicy tale to relate concerning the family of her arch-enemy? She advanced determinedly on the couple, already savouring the piquancy of a rousing victory over Mrs Penelope Beaumont.

Mark propelled Emily forward. She understood perfectly the instruction in his firm guidance and did her part by quickening her pace and keeping her bonnet brim low to shield her features.

Violet put on a spurt, and the exertion served her well. Suddenly she got a proper look past those powerful shoulders that, preposterously, were almost as wide as the corridor. 'Why…Miss Beaumont, is it not?' she purred. 'How are you, my dear? And how is your mama? Is she here with you?'

Emily stood rigid and tongue-tied for a moment. Obliquely a corner of her mind registered that she was hopelessly, irrevocably compromised. But she turned slowly to receive Mrs. Pearson's horribly gloating look. 'No, she is not,' Emily said in a lightly quavering tone.

'Oh…I see,' Violet said, immeasurable insinuation conveyed by those few words. Barely containing her glee, she added sweetly, 'I expect you heard me say to Mr Hunter that we are off to the Festival in Guildford. Are you going there? Or are you also travelling back to London?'

Emily moistened her lips, about to speak, but Violet piped up again. 'If your parents are not here, I expect your brother is escorting you. No doubt Tarquin is somewhere about the place.' She gave an exaggerated peer about as though she might spot the fellow lurking in a corner. 'Of course, I know you would not be here alone with Mr. Hunter…would you?'

'Miss Beaumont is travelling with me,' Mark interjected coolly. He gave the woman a purely cynical stare. 'Enjoy the Festival, won't you…'

'Indeed I shall,' Violet said. She twitched a smile, and her skirts, in a travesty of respect. Even a blast of cold air as the couple went out into the night could not shift her. She stood for some minutes shivering in the draught, a wondrously smug smile on her thin countenance.

'She is a malicious witch and will delight in making trouble for our family.' Emily's face fell forward into her cupped palms. 'Oh, why did I ever set out today on such a stupid mission? Everything is now so much worse!' she wailed.

The curricle sped on through the night, but one of Mark's hands relinquished the reins to slide about Emily's shoulders and draw her close against his side. A thumb smoothed against a wind-chilled cheek, back and forth in soothing rhythm until she succumbed to his comfort. A small hand snaked about his waist and she clung uninhibitedly to him, her eyes screwed tight against the breeze and burning tears.

'Hush…' Mark said softly. 'You did what you thought best, and your brother is fortunate to have a sister as loyal and caring as you.' The equipage raced smoothly on as he encouraged her head against his shoulder.

Emily snuggled readily into the lee of his powerful body, a watery snuffle muffled against his coat. 'My intention was to shield my parents from further distress! Now look what I have done! I have increased their troubles tenfold!' She miserably shook her head back and forth. 'A wayward son is one thing. Society will tolerate a young man sowing wild oats, but not the shameless behaviour of his unmarried sister.'

'Hush, Emily.' Mark dropped his face to hers,

nudging up her chin so he might touch together their lips. She tasted salty-sweet and he relinquished her mouth reluctantly to concentrate on the dark road. 'It is not insurmountable. There are ways and means of putting this right…'

'There's only one way and you know it.' Emily choked on a hysterical giggle. 'We must announce we are to be married. And I think you know far too much about me now to ever want to do that!'

Chapter Fifteen

'You are a selfish wretch!'

'I know…I'm sorry,' Tarquin mumbled whilst shamefacedly contemplating his bitten nails. He suddenly leaned across the breakfast table, snatching at his sister's hands to impress on her his apology.

Emily shrank back, firmly crossing her arms over her waist as though to prevent him again touching her. 'Do you comprehend the extent of the chaos you caused?' A whirling hand illustrated the magnitude of it all. Emily tipped back her head in despair.

Of course she already knew the answer to that! Her brother was ignorant of a great deal of the damage that had resulted from his foolishness. The worst of which was her horribly inopportune meeting with Violet Pearson, and the ruinous effect it might have on their whole family. There was much she must tell Tarquin, and ask him, but she could barely contain her temper well enough to talk to him at all. With a depressive sigh Emily turned her attention on the coffee pot. She poured a cup and immediately gulped a mouthful of the strong, bitter brew.

'Have you yet told our parents of your real reason for running away? Sooner or later it is bound to come out. You cannot keep your wife hidden for ever.' Emily had breathed the final sentence in an undertone whilst darting a wary look at the door. She hoped they had not been overheard.

Her mother was no doubt still abed; it was not yet her usual time for rising. She was confident her father would already be out on matters of business, for he was an early bird however late he retired. But servants had a knack of gleaning titbits to chew over below stairs.

Emily again thanked her lucky stars that she had got home yesterday just minutes before her parents returned from their evening's entertainment. She had been halfway up the stairs when she heard a key in the lock, followed by their jolly conversation in the hallway. Despite her weariness Emily had instinctively sprinted up the remaining treads and out of sight. Concealing herself behind the banisters on the landing, she had called her goodnights in a sleepy voice as though she had kept awake especially to do so. Trudging off to bed, she had felt quite guilty at her spontaneous subterfuge, and then quite silly too. Forlornly she had recalled that, if Violet Pearson were bent on making mischief, her hellish jaunt with Riley would eventually be uncovered no matter how good had been her play-acting.

Emily's attention returned to Tarquin. She was still waiting to learn from him whether their parents were cognizant of the fact of their son's scandalous marriage.

'Jenny is dead,' Tarquin blurted out. His eyes glittered as he added sombrely, 'And she was not really my wife at all.'

Emily clattered her cup and saucer together and her lips parted in astonishment. 'Jenny is *dead*?' she echoed in a husky whisper. 'And you say you did *not* marry her?' She clamped a hand to her brow and thumb and forefinger pressed indentations into pearly skin. 'Was it all for nothing? Did you suspect all along the marriage was some sort of hoax?'

'No! I believed we were legally leg-shackled, I swear.' Tarquin concealed his trembling lips with a fist planted hard against them, only removing it to briefly enlighten Emily to the circumstances of poor

Jenny's demise at the hands of the fiendish Riley. He cleared his throat to gruffly continue, 'Jeremiah Plumb is a clergyman, if a shifty character. It all seemed correct. The marriage was certainly con-summated…' Tarquin blinked nervously and blushed on recalling to whom he was expressing his thoughts.

'Go on,' Emily prompted, dismissing his tacit apology as unnecessary.

'Jenny regained consciousness for a short while after Mark set out to rescue you. She told me be-fore she expired that I was not her only husband. It was Riley's idea, of course, to make of her a bigamist. At one time I think she was quite infatu-ated with him. But she came to know him for a selfish, avaricious swine.' Tarquin flung his spine against the chair back. 'Riley had successfully ex-torted money from other fellows who had been tricked into taking vows when stewed. Once sober, they readily parted with cash to seal Riley's lips.'

'He thought you would too. But you had none to give.'

Tarquin nodded slowly. 'So he had the confounded cheek to accost you instead for payment.' His mouth thinned to a white line. 'I would gladly murder the brute for that alone, never mind what he did to Jenny!'

'And in doing so most definitely embroil us all in a terrible brouhaha.' Emily pointed out angrily. 'We are not yet over one calamity before you are talking of creating another.'

Tarquin hung his head. 'I shall arrange for a decent burial for Jenny in any case,' he murmured on a suspiciously watery gurgle. 'She wasn't wholly a bad girl.'

Angry as Emily was with Tarquin, he deserved her sympathy for his bereavement. Kneeling close to his chair, she looked up into his mournful damp countenance. 'I'm so very sorry to hear about Jenny's fate. Had I known earlier, I would not have scolded you so.' Her pale fingers covered his, squeezed in comfort. 'It's a mess and no doubt about it. But I'm glad to know you cared for one another. Jenny could have gone to her grave saying nothing about the bigamy, but she chose instead to put your mind at rest over it all. She loved you back, Tarquin,' she stressed softly.

Tarquin nodded and made a snuffling noise before cuffing at his nose.

Emily let him be and sank back on her heels. Her brother was deeply upset by the death of his illicit wife. Tarquin had fallen for a harlot, a woman who had conspired to trick him, but had ultimately risked and sacrificed her own life to help him. Emily felt no disgust on knowing on whom her brother had chosen to bestow his love. In fact, she rather admired him for having the pluck to buck convention in choosing his mate. She now suspected that, at the altar, her brother had been more in possession of his faculties than he cared to admit. Oddly that gave Emily a sense of serenity.

Gracefully she gained her feet and paced to the window. She stared out into a beautiful spring morning. The sun was shining and her countenance tilted up to be warmed by its golden glow. The lime trees were more leaf than wood, for the buds were now almost fully unfurled. With a sigh Emily turned her back on the pleasant scene. 'Will you tell our parents about the real reason for your disappearance?'

Tarquin shook his head. 'I am a widower—legal or not—and it is pointless now worrying them with news of a dead daughter-in-law.'

'Indeed,' Emily quietly concurred. She paced restlessly, then shot her brother a helpless look. 'I'm afraid to say there might soon be something even worse to disturb them.' For the first time that morning she allowed herself to ponder on her own distressing predicament. How long a reprieve might she have before Violet Pearson returned to town to ruin her future?

Just a day ago—it seemed so much longer than that!—she had written a letter to Stephen Bond in which she had kindly let him know she would only ever consider him a good friend. She had acted from altruism; now she felt mean for being relieved the note remained undelivered and in her cloak pocket.

But what would she do? Would she find the gall to encourage Stephen to propose simply to protect her reputation? That would certainly prove Sarah's hints on her woeful character correct: she *was* selfish and inconsiderate.

If her betrothal were official before Mrs Pearson returned to town, would the woman admit defeat and say nothing? More importantly, if whispers *did* start to circulate about her being spotted in scandalous circumstances with a bachelor, would Stephen renege on the contract? He would have every right to do so!

'I can't guess at it. You must explain what you mean,' Tarquin prompted.

With a sigh Emily proceeded to do so.

'Violet Pearson! Of all people!' Tarquin snorted in disgust. 'I don't socialise much with you ladies, but even I know that the old hag will go out of her way to stir the cauldron where our family is concerned.' The palms of his hands made forceful contact with his thighs. 'What the deuce was Hunter thinking of, taking you, unchaperoned, to an inn where you might be spotted together? I'll have something to say to him when I see him, I can tell you.'

A gasp of astonished laughter was Emily's first response to that. '*You* will have something to say to *him*?' she echoed incredulously. 'It might have slipped your mind that in fact Mark was doing you and me a very great favour by getting involved in any of this. If you think sensibly on it, you will understand that pulling in to the Rose and Crown was a necessity, not an indulgence. Mark had risked the health of his animals by travelling many miles at full pelt. The poor things were on their last legs and, had we continued, I might never have been safely returned home at all.'

'Calm down!' Tarquin muttered. He knew he had deserved her tirade. 'I'd not see you overturned in a ditch rather than compromised.' Suddenly he gave a knowing chuckle. 'For a lady who, as I recall, didn't have a good word to say about a certain gentleman, you jumped to his defence pretty quickly *and* fiercely.'

Emily felt blood sting in her cheeks at that shrewd observation. 'And I have good reason to do so, as do you. Had Mark not turned up when he did, I might still be at Devlin's mercy, and it would be your fault!'

'Nothing for it, then,' Tarquin suddenly proclaimed in ringing tones. 'Hunter must marry you.'

Emily's gasp of bitter laughter was drowned by the sound of the door opening. Millie was hovering on the threshold of the morning room.

'A visitor for you, Miss Emily,' the maid advised, her tone displaying her surprise that a caller had arrived at such an unfashionably early hour. 'Mr Hunter is in the hall.'

After a moment of breathless indecision Emily shot a fleeting glance at Tarquin. Her brother had a smug grin on his face. 'Show him in please, Millie,' she said faintly.

On learning the identity of her visitor Emily had sensed her heart cease to beat. Now it began to throb alarmingly. Of course, she had expected he would come today to speak to her about what had happened at the inn, but she had not expected him yet and was certainly not ready to receive him.

She crossly reminded herself that, had she not made that stupid remark last night, when tired and hysterical, she might not be so flustered by his arrival.

Mark had received her impulsive jest with unsmiling gravity. His taciturn visage had remained unflinchingly facing the road ahead as he urged the horses to increase pace. The final leg of the journey home to Mayfair had passed in virtual silence.

Surely he had not thought she seriously expected him to propose marriage? As though she would! She knew he was in love and spoken for. The attention he had paid to her was simply opportunistic flirting…she knew that too…

What had alarmed him, and turned her weak joke sour, was that they both had known she had voiced what others would think. If a genteel spinster were to be unfortunately compromised by a gentleman, polite society would deem it his duty to protect her reputation with an offer of marriage. But of course it was different with them. The gentleman had already guessed that the spinster was not as virtuous as polite society assumed her to be, and was loath to make the sacrifice.

'He's here to rescue your reputation, I'm sure.'

Tarquin's hissed encouragement caused Emily to cast on him a frown. Far from being here to ask her to be his wife, Emily guessed Mark Hunter's early arrival was due to his keenness to impress on her he knew the phrase about closing the stable door after the horse had bolted. And how could she blame him for that? For his pains, he risked being vilified as her heartless seducer rather than her saviour.

Looking quite heartbreakingly handsome, and the epitome of composure too, Mark strolled in to the room. He was so elegantly groomed—charcoal tailcoat, snow-white cravat and top boots gleaming like glass—that it was obvious he deemed this visit a matter of grave importance. His immaculate appearance reminded Emily that she had been too agitated by recent events to take much time with her toilette that morning. Tendrils of blonde hair were quickly smoothed back from her pearly brow and her pink dimity skirts were given an unobtrusive shake to neaten them.

Mark looked straight at her and she gave him a small smile, hoping to reassure him that he would not suffer on her account. He was a kind and decent man, she knew that now, and she would set him free to marry the woman he loved.

Emily's smile faded away for, far from being well received, her wordless welcome had caused his expression to become faintly ironic.

Tarquin immediately strode towards his friend and stuck out a hand. 'Good to see you, Mark.' The greeting was stressed in throbbing tones that conveyed a multitude of gratitude.

After a momentary hesitation Mark met the proffered hand. 'You'll forgive me if I don't return the compliment.' He managed to extricate his hand from being vigorously pumped. 'In fact, it would not bother me if I never set eyes on you again, Beaumont.'

Tarquin had the grace to turn florid. 'Caused a bit of trouble, I know…' he mumbled and hung his head.

'You have a nice way with understatement.' Mark's response was silky with sarcasm. 'Jenny?' It was a blunt question.

Tarquin's chin dropped further towards his chest. He shook his head.

'I'm very sorry,' Mark said quietly. Within a moment he followed that with, 'I would like to speak privately to your sister.'

Tarquin's lowered eyes batted between the couple and he cleared his throat. 'Yes…of course… understand…' he mumbled, backing towards the door. Emily received a sly wink from her brother before he slunk into the corridor.

'Ah…I see he does understand,' Mark commented drily as soon as the door had closed.

Emily nodded jerkily, inwardly cursing her brother for having made it seem that there was a conspiracy between them. 'I've just told him about the unfortunate meeting with Mrs Pearson…' Her voice faded into awkward silence.

'My apologies for calling at such an ungodly hour,' Mark said. 'I hoped to catch your father at home. I know he rises early.'

'He rises very early,' Emily echoed faintly.

Mark walked closer and Emily felt her stomach somersault, for his presence held undeniable allure. She had grown used to being welcomed into his arms, kissed and caressed until her worries evaporated and he was the mainstay of her existence. She clasped her hands tight behind her back, though she ached to rush to him, have him again make everything right. She backed away a step on realising with anguished sorrow that there was actually nothing she would like better than to become Mark Hunter's wife.

'You know why I am here, Emily,' Mark began levelly.

'Yes…' Emily began. 'And before you say more, there is something you ought to know…'

'Indeed there is,' he confirmed quietly. 'A couple of my questions remain unanswered. I have managed to work out the answer to one of those myself. When you first arranged to meet Riley on Whiting Street you were loitering in the lawyer's office to avoid Devlin, were you not?'

Emily merely gave a little nod. 'And the other?' she asked quickly, keen to get to the crux of the matter and set him free.

'I asked you once why you rebuffed my compliment on your innocence. I'm still waiting for your explanation.'

She had not at all anticipated that abrupt demand. The words that had been ready to release him blocked her throat. Her small tongue tip darted to moisten lips that felt arid. 'I think you know why I said it,' Emily blurted. Silver eyes that had been shielded by twin fans of dusky lashes suddenly sparked at him, proud and challenging.

'I imagine it is to do with the *passionate fondness* that Devlin says you shared.'

Emily tilted her chin a little higher. 'You are very astute, sir.'

'How passionately fond of him were you?'

'As passionately fond as it is possible to be,' Emily answered in a hoarse little voice. 'And we need not speak in riddles. You will not offend my delicate sensibilities by speaking of carnal love.' She suddenly unclasped her hands and brought them in front of her, flexing fingers that felt stiff with cramp. 'I think you have guessed that I lay with Nicholas when we were engaged. I am not a virgin,' she quickly continued in a whisper, 'And I do not want you to feel obliged to protect me with an offer of marriage…if indeed that was your intention.' She slid him a fleeting look and noted his expression was unreadable. His stillness, his silent unflinching regard, made her desperately seek something else to say.

'It is as well you have not found my father at home, if indeed your intention was to discuss a marriage contract. But you have not wasted your time in coming here,' she intrepidly continued, despite his refusal to participate in the conversation. 'You no doubt feel an unwelcome duty has been thrust upon you. Rest assured it has not, and speaking to my father is quite unnecessary.' Emily walked to the breakfast table and began to stack the used crockery. A fork escaped her nervous clutch and clattered on to mahogany. She gave up the task and gripped the table edge instead. 'It was most unfortunate that our brief rest at the inn was witnessed, and by such a spiteful person. But there is no need for you to feel you must act to protect my good reputation.' Emily closed her eyes, willing him to speak. Any reaction…even a scornful observation that she had no good reputation to lose…would be better than his wordless audience. 'I have a gentleman friend,' she battled on. 'And he reciprocates my fond feelings.

It is now the right time for things between us to be made official.' Her silver-blue eyes were slowly raised to Mark's face.

'And you think that Stephen Bond would take to wife a wanton?'

Emily felt her complexion heating beneath his potent blue gaze. 'I do not think that our being spotted together will merit such harsh gossip being bandied about.'

'I think you know I didn't mean that.'

Emily's pink cheeks darkened to scarlet. 'Stephen will never know about that…unless you or Nicholas tell him.'

'Of course he will,' Mark jeered softly. 'He'll know the first time he lays with you…' He suddenly shot her a fierce look. 'Or perhaps he already has,' he murmured. 'Do you have a similar *passionate fondness* for Mr Bond? Or was it simply the thought of being a Viscountess that excited you?'

Chapter Sixteen

'How dare you!'

Emily felt her stomach writhe with humiliation, but stalked away from the table to face him indignantly. 'I was very young when I first fell in love and allowed Nicholas to seduce me.' She gulped in a steadying breath. 'I bitterly regret being duped by his lies, but I am no longer that silly, naïve child.' Her blonde head was flung back and she levelled on him quite a haughty look. 'You are hardly a model of virtue, and have a devil of a nerve to moralise! I wonder if Mrs Emerson realises how fickle you are.'

'Whether she does or not is of no consequence,' he coolly replied.

'And that validates my opinion of your character,'

Emily breathed. 'That you would show so little respect for the feelings of the woman you love is disgraceful.'

Mark laughed, a guttural sound of raw sarcasm that sent a shiver through Emily.

'You have no idea what you are talking about, Miss Beaumont, and I suggest you leave alone the matter of my love affairs.'

'Gladly!' Emily snapped, but still smarting from his rebuke. 'If you will do the same for me.'

Their combative gazes locked for an infinite moment. Emily looked away first when he made no move to take his leave.

'There is no need for you to stay longer,' she said stiffly. 'If a shred of conscience over my future is delaying you, let me put your mind completely at ease. I think you know I have little liking for you. I would not marry you if the only alternative was earning my keep on the streets.'

'I'm sure Devlin would be your keenest customer. He knows you suit the work,' Mark drawled, a twitch of a smile his only reaction to her gasp of outrage. But beneath his blasé exterior bubbled uncontrollable jealousy. His fears had been realised: the woman with whom he'd fallen in love had slept with a man he detested. But even if mild-mannered Stephen Bond had taken her virginity, he would have liked it no better. A primeval need to have been the first to possess her would not be denied, and was making him callous. 'You might not like me, sweetheart,' he said, 'but what does that matter? We both know we can forgo fondness and concentrate on passion.'

Emily felt her skin heating and she swung away from him, desperate to formulate a rebuttal. What he'd intimated about their compatibility was cruel, but none the less true. Even before she knew her feelings towards him were changing, she had sensed the potent allure of his virility. His mocking eyes were scorching her profile, his scathing words were echoing in her ears, yet still she craved the relief of the bittersweet sensuality he could arouse in her.

She was the one who hadn't been entirely honest. At one time she might have persuaded herself she did not like Mark Hunter; but she could not do it any more. Despite his insults, she knew she most certainly did like him. In fact, she feared she had fallen in love with him. But she'd never accept being Mark's despised wife any more than she had once wanted to endure the humiliation of Nicholas marrying her under duress. Before Mrs Pearson returned from the music festival, another solution must be found.

'Would you like me to prove to you how good

we'd be together, Emily? It'll be my pleasure to drive any thoughts of Devlin from you...'

Emily felt a *frisson* pass through her; the imagery he'd purposely put in her mind had sent iced fire streaking through her veins. Slow footfalls approached, then firm fingers were skimming the silken skin of her arms. Warm, intoxicating lips stroked her nape, slid to the sensitive hollow behind an ear. Her head angled to accommodate him, and she luxuriated in the fever he'd so easily raised in her blood. But she steeled herself against succumbing to his practised seduction. He wanted her, but deemed her of easy virtue, and was unabashed to tell her so. Desire could be enchanting, but without love and respect it was worthless to her. She had learned that bitter lesson with Nicholas.

Anticipating her imminent rejection, Mark released her, denying her even that small proud triumph. He moved away to brace a foot against the fender, a hand against the stone chimneypiece. With thoughtful nonchalance he steadily regarded her. 'Once your parents discover from Violet Pearson what has gone on, they'll be desperate to get you settled with the first man who'll have you.' He stooped, scooped up a log and lobbed it on to the embers in the grate. 'Trust me, Stephen Bond won't be applying to be your husband. He might be smitten, he might even consider a less binding arrangement with you, but he'll not risk losing his grandmother's inheritance by taking a discredited woman to wife. Once Violet spreads her poison he'll be a laughing-stock, and Augusta won't allow shame to taint their family's name.'

Emily flinched from the unpalatable truth. Augusta had openly told her she didn't think her right for her grandson; and this had been whilst the woman believed her reputation to be intact! Mrs Bond would never sanction her grandson's marriage to Miss Beaumont after she heard the scandalous rumours. Dejectedly Emily had to agree with Mark's interpretation of Stephen's character: he would not buck convention, or his inheritance, for her sake.

Having rekindled the fire Mark strolled to the door, rested back against it with his arms crossed over his chest. For a long, almost unbearable moment he subjected her to his sleepy scrutiny. 'I'll consider marrying you, sweetheart,' he said eventually. 'Not because I feel obliged to do so, but because I suspect there are sweet advantages to taking a wanton bride.'

'Was that Mark Hunter I glimpsed in the vestibule a moment ago? My, he's quick off the mark this morning! But then I fear he must have pressing matters on his mind concerning the conduct of that scapegrace son of mine.'

Penelope Beaumont sailed into the parlour, her pastel morning dress wafting about her trim ankles. 'Where *is* Tarquin, by the by? Is he in hiding from his friend's scolding?'

Emily's silence prompted Penelope to take a proper look at her daughter. Noticing the strain etched into her white features, she hurried immediately to her side. 'Whatever is the matter, Emily? You look dreadful.' Penelope gasped and put a hand to her throat. 'Never say that Mr Hunter has upset *you*? It's Tarquin who deserves his complaints!'

Penelope suddenly looked askance at her daughter. Over the years she had cringed on more than one occasion when Emily had been snappish with Mark Hunter. Previously she had marvelled at the way the fellow tolerated it with equanimity. If Emily had caught the sharp side of his tongue at last, perhaps it was no more than she deserved. 'Were you rude to him, Emily?'

Emily was about to deny any such thing, but instead forced a fist against her mouth as she was racked with hysterical giggles.

'For goodness' sake, Emily!' Mrs Beaumont

chided. 'Is it not enough that we have a son who makes a habit of acting foolishly?' In exasperation her shawl was yanked this way and that about her shoulders. 'And Mr Hunter is such an influential gentleman, too. I was hoping that you might persuade him to continue to be Tarquin's good friend. Mark always seemed to have a soft spot for you despite your petulance.' Penelope stamped to the door, then whisked about on the threshold to deliver a parting shot. 'I'm off to do some shopping and I'd sooner go alone.'

Immediately after her mother went out Emily sought the sanctuary of her chamber. But even the comfort of a little nap was to be snatched away. Her brother had soon stationed himself outside the door and begun cajoling to be allowed in to talk to her. Her refusal had prompted him to direct hissed questions through the keyhole. Was he to have Hunter as a brother-in-law? he'd repeatedly demanded to know. Or was a scandal going to break next week when the Pearson woman came back to town?

Emily had lain on her bed with her hands covering her face. She'd felt too enervated and emotional to again wrangle with any one else that morning, so she simply ignored Tarquin. Eventually he had mumbled about funeral arrangements for Jenny and gone away. From her window Emily had just watched her brother striding off purposefully up the street. About to try and again seek sweet oblivion in a catnap, she instead decided she too would go out. Perhaps the air might revive her numb mind and bring fresh ideas to lighten her depression.

She had not seen Sarah for some days and craved to have an uncomplicated chat to a friend. And why should she not try and enjoy the little interlude left to her? In a short while, when Mrs Pearson returned from Guildford, all would be deadly serious. Momentarily Emily hesitated by the front door and smoothed her gloves with agitated fingers. If she visited Sarah, Stephen Bond was sure to be a topic of conversation between them. Emily was unsure what to say about him any more. With a sigh she lightly descended the steps and headed off in the direction of Sarah's house. She would negotiate a path across rickety bridges when she encountered them! Drawing in an invigorating gulp of crisp air, she quickened her pace.

'It's good to see you, Emily.' Sarah rose from where she had been working on her embroidery and rushed to meet her friend. She took both Emily's hands in her own.

Emily returned her friend's enthusiastic welcome

by squeezing her fingers. She was glad that there was no hint of the awkwardness that had been present when last they had parted company.

'Come…sit down. I'll arrange for tea,' Sarah said, already halfway to the bell pull. 'Papa said that he'd heard your brother is back in town,' she said conversationally. 'That must be a relief for you all.' She sat close to Emily and bestowed a sympathetic look. 'Is it a relief, or has he simply brought his woes back with him?'

About to prevaricate on that tricky subject, Emily was saved the need to do so. Mrs Harper was framed in the parlour doorway.

'Oh, hello, Emily, my dear. How nice to see you. I didn't realise you had a visitor, Sarah. Are you going to accompany me? Or would you now rather not as Emily is arrived? I have not said definitely that you *will* attend…'

'Definitely, I will not, thank you all the same, Mama,' Sarah returned with a little conspiratorial smile for Emily.

'Oh…please…do not let me stop you going out,' Emily said at once. 'I can call another day.' She began to rise.

'No! I insist you stay!' Sarah cried and clutched at Emily's arm to make her again sit down.

Mrs Harper gave the young ladies a blithe smile and, with a little wave, withdrew.

Sarah turned to Emily, a hand dramatically placed upon her breast. 'Don't abandon me, please! I was ready to summon up a migraine to avoid the ordeal of weak tea and stale Madeira cake. Of course, that sour-faced old biddy makes me feel quite bilious too.'

Emily stripped off her gloves and settled back into the cushions of the sofa. For the first time in many hours she felt good humour ease the painful constriction in her chest. 'And which poor hostess, pray, has earned your wicked description?' Emily feigned thoughtfulness. 'I can think of many who the cap might fit, but you must enlighten me, lest I insult one of your mother's best friends.'

Sarah wove her needle into cloth to secure it then pushed away the tambour. She made herself comfortable, crossing her arms, before beginning, 'Violet Pearson has forgone her trip to Guildford and returned to town. No sooner is she back than she has arranged to have everyone to tea.' Sarah gave a chuckle, oblivious to her friend's stricken expression on hearing her yarn. 'Mama said the Pearsons are famous misers and there will be only one reason Violet has squandered the cost of the journey *and* paid out to entertain the moment she is home: the woman has discovered something riveting and is determined to be first with a juicy bit of gossip!'

For the second time in a week Geoffrey Lomax gawped at his master's broad back and wondered what had put the fellow again in such a foul temper. Moments before Mark had entered the house and proceeded past him towards his study with just a terse greeting emerging from between his teeth.

The butler watched him and shrugged in despair. He had been about to announce to Mr Hunter that he had a visitor, but possessed neither nimble legs to run to catch up with him, nor the vulgarity to shout the information in his wake. Let him discover for himself that his brother was in the house waiting to see him.

Mark came upon Sir Jason warming himself, inside and out, with his cognac and his fire.

'You look comfortable,' Mark drawled sardonically.

Jason glanced up from his hearthside chair and stretched his long legs out in front of him. 'Do you begrudge me my contentment?' he asked bluntly.

Mark gave his brother a quirk of a smile. Did he resent Jason's contentment? No…but most certainly he coveted it. Just a short while ago he would have pitied his brother the loss of his bachelorhood. But that was before Emily Beaumont had gazed at him with those captivating silver eyes and asked for his help in finding her brother. Now he was enslaved, heart and soul, and he wished he were not. Mark abruptly clashed together the decanter and a glass. Remembering his manners, he held out the bottle.

Jason declined another drink. He watched as his brother dropped into the chair opposite, and proceeded to sink the cognac in a single gulp.

Mark had been acting oddly for some time, and Jason had come here to discover if his wife's suspicions were correct. Lady Hunter had ordered her husband to bring Mark back to dine with them that evening, but first Jason deemed a little private chat might benefit.

Helen was sure Mark and Emily Beaumont were, despite evidence to the contrary, falling in love. Jason knew better than to gainsay his wife on such matters of excellent female intuition. But, on the occasions they had all been in company together, Jason had noticed Emily had seemed cool with Mark rather than enthralled. At Fiona Gerrard's recent soirée, the couple had spent time alone, but Jason had put that down to a necessarily discreet conversation concerning that numbskull brother of hers.

Mark was staring unblinking into the fire, and

Jason gave his moody countenance a more penetrating appraisal. He knew from personal experience that the road to love and happiness could be strewn with pitfalls, and his brother certainly appeared to be licking his wounds.

'Helen has sent me to fetch you back for dinner. And she won't take no for an answer,' Jason added when he noticed Mark considering his response. An excuse was imminent.

'Who else?'

Jason grinned—he knew exactly why his brother was suspicious. In the past Helen had been known to seat her eligible brother-in-law close to nubile young ladies of her acquaintance. 'No matchmaking, I swear,' Jason promised. 'It's just the three of us. Helen is concerned that we have seen little of you lately. What have you been up to?'

Mark watched his empty glass as it oscillated between thumb and forefinger. Abruptly he rose and refilled it. 'I've been courting.' The announcement was followed by a grunt of mirthless laughter. Mark thumped his glass down on the desk. 'That's what I've been doing. And I really don't think that tonight I feel sociable.'

'Damned tricky business,' Jason commiserated, settling a booted foot on a knee. 'Wouldn't want to do it again myself.' He gave Mark a rueful look. He knew his brother recalled the obstacles that had complicated his relentless pursuit of Helen Marlowe. 'Do you want to tell me about it?'

'No.' Mark strolled about his desk and picked up a few papers to idly scan them.

'I take it the lady has declined your kind offer, in which case it isn't Barbara you've settled on. She'd meet you at the church tomorrow.'

'You're being damned inquisitive,' Mark snarled. 'Thank Helen very much for her invitation, but—'

'I'm being your brother,' Jason interjected quietly. 'I know something is not right and I don't like to see you unhappy, but if you don't want to talk about it…' He shrugged. 'It's your business.' Jason gained his feet and looked squarely into Mark's eyes. 'I've done my best; the least you can do is return the compliment. If I turn up without you, it's likely I'll have to endure some nagging, and a very lonely night.'

'The joys of married life?' Mark suggested drily.

'Indeed,' Jason replied. 'But it won't put you off any more than it did me. If you love her, you'll take that and more…'

'I really think I ought to be going.' Emily had sat chatting with Sarah for forty endless minutes before she felt able to issue that statement. Since she had learned of Violet Pearson's aborted trip to Guildford she had subdued her agitation and attempted to maintain a façade of cheeriness. But for her good manners preventing it, she would have quit Sarah's company five minutes after having been invited to sit down and take tea.

She had instinctively decided not to confide in her friend her grave suspicions over what had brought Violet haring back to town. When Mrs Harper returned from taking afternoon tea, Sarah would know it all, and so would many others in polite society. This evening, salons and drawing rooms throughout London would be abuzz with gossip… concerning her!

Sarah gave her friend a searching look. She was aware that Emily's mood had changed after her tale about the Pearson woman. 'Have I said something to upset you? I wouldn't have spoken unkindly about Violet if I thought you liked her…'

Emily forced a gasp of laughter. 'Heavens above, I do not! You *know* I do not.'

Sarah frowned in puzzlement, but leaned forward to pick up the teapot. 'Have some more tea,' she cajoled.

Emily deposited on the table her cup and saucer

with a hand that shook and made the china rattle. 'I will not, thank you.'

Noticing that Sarah looked rather hurt, she added quickly. 'It is nothing you have said or done, Sarah, I swear. I…it is just…you are right…' she breathed with some relief as she recalled something her friend had mentioned earlier '…the return of the prodigal has not been without its worries. Tarquin would not be Tarquin if he turned up completely free of woes.'

Sarah took Emily's hands in her own and lightly pecked her cheek. 'I understand, but come again soon.'

Emily walked swiftly in the direction of home, but, at the corner of Callison Crescent, and with her door in sight, she stopped. What was she going to do? Would she go to her chamber and hide her head under the covers until tomorrow her name…her family's name…was dragged through the mud? She had thought Tarquin an unfit sibling to their young brother, Robert. How she was humbled for having deemed herself superior!

She had rashly assumed she had time to decide on a course of action. That buffer had now been whipped away and she was teetering on the brink of disaster. With a sob welling in her throat, she leaned back against a brick wall for support. She ignored curious looks from people busily traversing back and forth on the pavement and forced her mind to reflect on the only man who might be her saviour.

She had received a marriage proposal of sorts from Mark Hunter and simple pride had stopped her grabbing the opportunity. The half-hearted offer had been prompted by duty, and from his desire to make love to her. But how could she bear that? As his wife she would be safe from scourging tongues, but she could never bear the hurt of knowing her absent husband had spent the night with his mistress. She might have his name, but Barbara Emerson would have his love.

Emily smeared the wet from her eyes and blinked into the breeze. There was only one person she could talk to when she was so low.

Helen would not judge her. They were similar souls. Before she had married Sir Jason, the young widow, Helen Marlowe, had been forced to put at jeopardy her good name. Helen was no stranger to the risk of being ostracised.

Plunging her cold hands into her pockets, Emily turned and walked back the way she had come, heading towards Grosvenor Square.

Chapter Seventeen

'**I**'m very well, thank you, Cedric,' Emily glibly lied.

Old Cedric cocked his good ear at the visitor to discover how she fared. He had no need to ask her business, or her name. He knew very well that Miss Beaumont had come for a chat with her good friend Lady Hunter. He ushered her into the vast marble hallway of Sir Jason's magnificent townhouse.

'And how are you?' Emily asked the old retainer.

The butler wagged his head up and down. 'Mustn't grumble…mustn't grumble.' Suddenly a look of enlightenment lifted his aged features. 'I've just remembered that Lady Hunter's maid went up to dress her hair. Dinner is quite soon.'

'Oh…I will not stop, then. I had not realised it was so late.' Emily sent a glance to a stately grandfather clock set against the wall and saw it was indeed almost a quarter to seven. She had lost all track of time since she'd left the house at late afternoon. It was well past the hour to pay an impromptu social call, even on a close friend. With an apologetic little smile for Cedric she turned to the door.

'Emily!'

A great deal of warmth and welcome was in that single word. Lady Hunter was gliding down a curving staircase, looking a vision of elegance in lemon silk with her ebony ringlets swept to one side of her lovely face.

Once on the marble tiles Helen hurried towards Emily and linked arms with her, drawing her further into the house.

'I will not stop, Helen. I had not realised quite how late it is, and you are dressed to dine.'

A hand flick dismissed that as of no importance. 'Of course you must stay! Jason is not even yet home.' Helen raised her eyes heavenward. 'He is probably taking a tipple with his brother. I know he was going to see Mark.' Helen watched carefully for a reaction to that idle information. With an amount of satisfaction she noted that a reference to Mark Hunter had indeed made Emily start. Helen also noticed that Emily's heart-shaped countenance was unusually wan, and shadows bruised the delicate skin beneath her eyes.

'Come along to the blue salon. It is just finished and you must tell me if you like the furnishings I have chosen.'

Emily looked about, praised her friend's excellent taste, then the ladies took seats close together on a sofa covered in fabric of blue and white stripes. Settled barely a moment, Helen made to spring up to ring for some refreshment.

'No, I will not, thank you, Helen.' Emily managed a small smile, and to restrain Helen from rushing to the bell. 'I am awash with tea. I have just been to see Sarah Harper,' she obliquely explained. The tenuous hold she had on her composure evaporated. A hand flew to her face to shield the gleam of tears.

'What is it?' Helen asked immediately, drawing her friend into a solicitous embrace. 'Surely Sarah has not upset you? I could tell straight away that all was not well.'

'It is not Sarah…leastways, nothing she has intentionally done. But she told me Mrs Pearson is already back in town and I can't bear it.'

Helen patted at her friend's quivering shoulders. 'I know she is a witch, but we can hide her broomstick.' Helen's gentle levity could not disguise that she had been made anxious by Emily's distress. Emily was an intrepid character and not prone to waterworks.

A gurgling laugh burst from Emily, but she remained quite still and uncommunicative, rallying the courage to relate her tale.

'Has Tarquin given the tabbies something new to relish?' Helen probed. 'I had heard he is back in town too.'

'A scandal *is* about to break. But it concerns me and I don't know what to do! My parents will be heartbroken.' Emily pressed a scrap of lace to her damp eyes.

'Hush…' Helen soothed. 'It cannot be so bad. Is my brother-in-law aware of it?' After a pause, Helen rephrased her question. 'Is Mark involved in any way?'

Emily gave an almost imperceptible nod.

'Start at the very beginning,' Helen urged softly.

Disengaging herself from Helen's arms, Emily sat straight and drew a gulp of a breath to begin her woeful account. She was interrupted before she had uttered one word.

'Just the three of us to dine this evening, I see…'

The sardonic male voice made both Emily and Helen turn simultaneously towards the door.

On the threshold stood two tall, immaculately attired gentlemen. One of them seemed as though he might pivot on his heel and leave rather than enter the room.

Mark Hunter was directing a look of extreme irony at his brother, Jason. His eyes then moved to Emily and lingered.

In response to his brother's tacit accusation, Jason gave a shrug, gesturing his bewilderment. But his eyes, when they shot to his wife, were brimming with quizzical amusement, and not a little admiration.

Helen sent her husband a welcoming smile, but it faded as she realised that Emily had jumped to her feet.

'I must go, Helen. I'm sorry to have troubled you,' Emily breathed, her face flaming. She had heard, and comprehended, the irony in Mark's tone. He imagined that Helen and she had plotted this meeting, and he had been lured back by his brother to be a target for their matchmaking. He suspected she had changed her mind, and was now so desperate to get him to issue a proper proposal that she had humbled herself to trap him.

She had been on the point of asking Helen's advice, but had already guessed what it would be. There was only one sensible course of action if she was to protect her family from shame: marry Mark Hunter if he would have her.

But all that was rational had been set to flight by his scorn and arrogance. Her spirits had rallied and she was sorely tempted to loose at him an immediate defence. Angry words teetered on her tongue tip. For two pins she would have told him that, had she known *he* was in the vicinity, she would have given Grosvenor Square a very wide berth indeed. But she would not demean herself with any such petty barbs. With her head high, she steadily paced towards the door.

'Do not disturb your plans for this evening, sir. I am leaving,' Emily said with cool politeness as she came nearer to him.

'Don't go on my account, Miss Beaumont.' Mark started into the room on a direct path to meet her.

Emily's pace slowed; they were on a collision course, but she would not give him the satisfaction of stepping aside. With barely a yard separating them she came to an abrupt halt.

Mark took another step until he was within arm's length of her bristling little figure.

Emily's chin was jerkily elevated, setting her blonde curls dancing. She gazed up into a face of raw-boned masculinity. Why did he always look so devastatingly attractive? She inwardly railed as she felt her body swaying towards him. Even now, with tension crackling between them, she yearned for his strength and comfort. Hastily she put all such thoughts from her mind. In a business-like fashion she started to pull on her gloves, wordlessly impressing on him he was delaying her. A soft noise prompted her to tilt her head to one side to see past him. The door had clicked shut on the discreet departure of Jason and Helen.

'Let me pass, please,' she demanded. 'I have to go. It is dinner time.'

'Which is surely why you're here.'

Rather miffed, Emily pointed out the glaring error in his assumption. 'I'm hardly dressed for the occasion,' she said stiffly, deliberately glancing down at her plain, serviceable ensemble.

Mark gave her attire a leisurely scrutiny. 'You look fine to me.' It was husky, complimentary.

'That remark shows how little you understand women,' Emily snapped with heightened pique.

'Amen to that,' he said on a dry laugh.

Emily moistened her lips, aware of peacock-blue eyes searing her face. Feeling overwhelmed by his closeness, she took a pace away. 'I know you believe this is no chance meeting,' she blurted. 'It is. I came here uninvited, and your brother and sister-in-law have done nothing underhand. They are not accomplices in some scheme to hook you, or in any way responsible for your embarrassment.'

'I'm not embarrassed. I am, however, intrigued as to why you pay your visits so late.'

Emily flicked up at him a bold stare. 'A pressing matter brought me here.'

'A pressing matter that concerns me?'

Emily felt blood flood beneath her cheeks. 'It's none of your business.'

'I think you know that's not true, Emily,' he lightly corrected. 'And what was Lady Hunter's advice? Should you grasp the nettle and marry me?'

'I might ask you the same question, sir,' Emily returned immediately. 'What was your brother's advice?'

'Jason doesn't know I asked you to be my wife.'

'Asked me to be your wife?' Emily echoed with husky scorn. 'Is that what you said to me?' Silver eyes flared at him. 'It sounded very much as though you were suggesting I be your…' She pressed together her lips, regretting having made herself sound vulgar. Quickly she made to dodge past him.

He moved to block her path. 'And you made it sound as though marriage to me would be a fate worse than death.'

Emily became still as a surge of remorse washed

over her. He had sounded hurt as well as angry. Her eyes fluttered shut as thoughts jumbled in her mind. Had she been so concerned with protecting her own pride that she had ignored the damage done to his? Mark always seemed so effortlessly self-contained, so invincible. She had rebuffed him brusquely, she knew, but had believed he must eventually welcome his release from an onerous duty to save her reputation. Suddenly she felt the tension seeping from her body.

'We should stop acting like petulant children,' she said quietly, barely flinching from the quizzical look that remark provoked. But she could tell that he, too, would welcome a truce.

They seemed on firmer ground, and Emily intended to tread carefully so they might equally debate the matters perturbing her. 'I know you would make Nicholas pay for what he has done, but I beg you will not worsen the situation by fighting him.'

Mark's lips twitched in a rueful smile. 'I won't say it wasn't my intention, but Riley got to him first. The fiasco ended in a scrap between them. Devlin is back home, and looking very much the worse for wear. The official report is that the Viscount was attacked by felons on the road.'

Emily's little gasp earned her a frown.

'Are you worried about him?'

Emily quickly shook her head. 'No! I hope his bruises are sore for weeks!' she announced pithily. 'But I fear his battered appearance might lead to inquisitiveness, and that might, in turn, lead to awkward questions.'

'He is lying low, and packing up his household to leave town. Ostensibly, his move to the country is due to his husbandly concern for the delicate condition of his wife.'

'It is no constitutional, I'm sure.' She gave Mark a tentative smile. 'You have made him go, have you not?' Quickly she added, 'I don't want to know how you brought it about.'

Mark's lids descended over his eyes. 'I simply suggested it might be wise. Devlin is not so stupid as to fail to understand that his behaviour could have grave repercussions. He knows Riley hates him, and would betray him for a pittance. Abduction and attempted rape carry heavy penalties, even for peers of the realm.'

Emily nodded slowly. 'And Riley?'

'I imagine he will make himself scarce rather than be dealt with by his cronies. They were not happy that Jenny was mortally injured. Her death will warrant an investigation and bring the authorities down on all their heads.' Mark looked at Emily and said softly, 'I am very sorry about what happened to her.'

'Tarquin is too,' Emily replied. 'I think he truly loved her at first and still does, despite knowing she was a bigamist…'

'A bigamist?' Mark echoed incredulously. 'They were not really wed at all?' Harshness was again present in his face and tone.

'He did not know until the end.' Emily quickly leaped to her brother's defence. 'Riley made Jenny wed those men so he might blackmail them. She told Tarquin all before she died. He is very upset to have lost her and you must not be angry with him over it or I will…' Her threats faded into silence.

'Or you will what?' Mark taunted softly. 'What will you do, Emily? Tackle his problems alone next time?'

Emily winced beneath his mockery. He had every right to go this minute and harangue her brother till kingdom come. 'He is different now,' she said quietly. 'I have never known my brother show such remorse. Usually he is too eager to find a gaming table to tarry long enough to say sorry.' She gazed up into Mark's eyes. 'I truly believe this awful episode has made him mend his ways.'

'I hope you're right,' Mark replied. 'It won't be before time.'

Emily drew in a quivering breath as the silence between them lengthened. For some minutes they had been concentrating on any issue but the one that truly mattered. Now it would no longer be denied. Emily knew it was time to surrender to her fate. To grasp the nettle, as he had said…

'Our squabbles are hindering us finding a solution to our own troubles.'

'There is only one solution, Emily, and you know what it is.' Impatiently he raked five fingers through his dark hair, ruining its neat appearance. 'A notice ought to be immediately gazetted. Time is running out…'

'It has run out,' Emily whispered. She raised her eyes to meet his, for they had immediately whipped to her face. 'Violet Pearson did not go to Guildford. She has returned instead to town, and I think I need not tell you why.'

Mark twisted a smile. 'So you have been denied even a few days' respite.'

'As have you.' Her gaze clung to his face as she said, 'I'm so sorry.' She moved a little closer, wistfulness puckering her perfect features. 'Had I not asked you to help me find Tarquin…had I not been foolish enough to go off alone with Riley…you would not now find yourself in such a terrible situation.'

Mark raised a hand, touched a single finger softly to her lips to silence her. Emily's lids drooped and for just a moment she revelled in the feel of his skin on hers. She took a deep breath and turned her face away. 'No…let me finish. There is much I must say. I have not thanked you for your help and, Heaven knows, you deserve my gratitude.'

'I don't want your gratitude, Emily,' Mark said hoarsely.

'I know you do not. Despite your angry words, I know you have given your aid freely, and would do so again.' She paused, thinking back over those years she had known Mark Hunter. For most of their acquaintance she had treated him coldly because of the incident surrounding her brother's imprisonment. In her heart she had known that her loyalty to Tarquin was extreme and unappreciated. Tarquin had been wild and out of control, and Mark had been right to rein him in. Difficult as it was to now eat humble pie, she must do it for her conscience's sake.

'I don't simply owe you my gratitude; I owe you an apology too.' She sensed smouldering eyes warming her. 'I know that when you had Tarquin sent to the Fleet you were being cruel to be kind. His incarceration stopped him gambling, and losing what little assets he had left. I was wrong to put the blame for it on you. I was wrong to be insolent to you.' Emily slanted a nervous peek at him through a web of long, inky lashes. 'Tarquin is lucky indeed you are still his friend, and that you have done so much recently to help him.'

'I didn't do it for him.'

Emily took a step closer to gauge his expression.

'I did it for you; surely you realised that?' he said gruffly.

Emily searched blue eyes that were devoid of irony, that seemed soulful, and intent on analysing her reaction to his words.

'Because you want to sleep with me?' Emily whispered.

'Because I love you, Emily Beaumont.' In a low, velvety voice he added, 'And, naturally, I want to prove that to you in bed.' He came purposefully closer. 'Actually, I'd like to prove it to you now.'

Hands that were lightly vibrating were raised to tenderly cup her bashful face and turn it up to his.

'You love me, even though you know that I lay willingly with Nicholas?' Emily asked in a small voice.

'I can't pretend I like knowing it,' Mark admitted with raw tenderness. 'I admit too that, since you told me, I've acted like a sulky youth over it.' His manner was endearingly self-conscious. 'I've always abhorred hypocrites, yet now I've acted as one.' His thumbs swept soft arcs on the satin skin of her jaw. 'I owe you an apology. It's not your fault that you were seduced by Devlin's lies and promises. You were young and sincere and understandably vulnerable to a master of deceit.' Mark paused. 'I don't like knowing that you gave him a precious part of yourself, or that you wanted to marry him. But perhaps you don't like knowing that, in my youth, I loved Barbara Emerson, and wanted her for my wife.'

Emily gazed at him with eyes that had spontaneously filled with prickling tears. 'I don't like knowing it at all. I don't like the rumours that you will wed. I don't like it that she is still your mistress.' She ended her admission on a shrill note of indignation that made Mark wryly smile.

'She isn't…not any more…' he soothed. 'I have seen Barbara today and told her that it is finished between us.' Mark was prevented from adding that he'd had no intention of asking Barbara to marry him since he turned twenty-one.

Emily suddenly flung her arms about his neck, hugging him chokingly tight. 'I thought you still loved her. I thought you hoped to marry her, and would hate me for depriving you of the woman you truly wanted as your wife.'

'You're the woman I truly want as my wife, Emily,' Mark told her gravely. His lips skimmed the silky blonde hair at her brow. 'We both have loved and wanted to marry people who we now know would have ultimately made us unhappy. We must be thankful that those affairs are behind us and we are free to concentrate on our future together.' He tilted up her chin with a single digit. 'Do you agree?'

Chapter Eighteen

'I do agree.'

'And Stephen Bond?'

'Stephen is a nice man, but I do not love him. In fact, I had a letter telling him so to post, but was distracted when Riley abducted me.' Emily gave him an adoring smile. 'I love you, Mark…so very much, and would be greatly honoured to be your wife.' She paused, raised a hand to tenderly cup his angular chin. 'I love you so much more than ever I loved Nicholas…'

'Prove it,' Mark demanded, his voice gruff with need.

Emily immediately complied. She went on tiptoe to press her soft warm lips against his. But he wanted more wooing than a coy salute. Gamely she teased him with little nipping kisses until, satisfied, he allowed her tongue to slip into his mouth to tangle with his.

With a guttural sound rasping in his throat, Mark lifted her up so their faces were level and he could fully enjoy her sweet seduction. From instinct, her legs immediately separated, wound about his thighs to clasp him possessively to her. Mark forgot about flirtatious games; he wanted her… His mouth stroked back and forth on soft, willing lips, plundered with savage sensuality until the kiss was so deep their faces were still.

Easily carrying his sensual prize, he strode swiftly to the nearest wall.

With blue watered silk at her back and Mark's hard powerful body keeping her effortlessly in place, Emily loosened her cloak. With her face still upturned to his and her mouth greedily taking the onslaught of his lips, she felt for her buttons. Unsteady fingers slowly loosened her bodice by touch alone. Mark raised his head, his eyes glowing with desire as he watched her small moving fingers. Deliberately Emily opened her chemise until the sides flapped away from her alabaster skin like small lapels. With her feverish gaze still meshed with his, she pulled down the soft cotton until it framed and supported her naked breasts, raising them close to his mouth.

Mark's eyes swooped to adore the lush, milky flesh offered up to him. His mouth slowly descended to take her invitingly slack lips in a slow, rewarding kiss that made her squirm delightedly.

Emily arched her back, rotated her hips faster against the rigid heat at his pelvis, wordlessly begging for him to soothe the aching need building within her feminine core.

With his body supporting hers, he used both hands to take his gift. Long, avaricious fingers began to reverentially stroke, pamper, shape the quivering flesh he was preparing to feast on. First one, then the other, blood-red nub thickened, stiffened beneath his skilful tongue as it leisurely trailed torment. When her aching flesh was almost unbearably hot and swollen Emily fought to contain the sob of pleasure tightening her throat. In delirium her head was thrown back, twisted from side to side in wordless denial, but the groan burst from her.

Mark covered her panting mouth with his to stop the feral sound from increasing in volume.

'Hush…' he whispered against her bruised lips, his tone throaty and amused. 'That was loud enough to bring old Cedric running, and he's deaf as a post.'

Emily tensed, then, in chagrin, her eyes screwed tight shut. The haze of sensuality drugging her was ebbing away and fiery embarrassment taking its place. She was a guest in an aristocrat's mansion, yet was acting like a dockside harlot. With a subdued shriek of shame she struggled to find her feet and her dignity. She pushed at Mark's shoulders, wriggled this way and that to try to make him set her down.

Emily's writhing now drew a guttural noise from Mark. Her attempt to recover her modesty was having the reverse effect to the one intended. His arms tightened about her, subduing her protests whilst his mouth relentlessly pursued hers.

'Oh…let me go, Mark,' Emily pleaded in anguish as his lips cornered hers. 'Do you suppose they heard? What must your brother think of me? Do you think they understood what we…that is…do you think they *know* what we're doing?' She turned to him, grasped his lean, angular jaw, then rushed her soft palms up and down on abrasive skin to hurry his reassurance.

Mark tore his eyes from the delectable sight of her nude bosom heaving just inches from his hungry mouth.

'What do *you* think of me?' Emily wailed softly. His desire had harshly tautened his features and she craved some tender affection from him. Did Mark think she had just proved herself a hussy rather than a fitting wife?

He looked deep into her stormy eyes; touched his lips to hers in a lightly teasing kiss. 'I'll show you what I think of you.' But instead of a renewed seduction, he gently lowered her to the ground. His hands drew together her chemise, her gaping bodice, and painstakingly refastened them. He then slipped a hand to his pocket and withdrew a jeweller's box. Carefully he prised open the lid and turned towards her his gift. A huge rose-cut diamond caught candle flame and sparked fire. 'I brought this with me this morning. I didn't have a chance to give it to you.'

Emily's sharply indrawn breath caught in her throat. For a moment she was so mesmerised by the magnificent betrothal ring that she forgot to be concerned about his expertise in deftly fastening a lady's undergarments.

Whilst Emily gazed upon her beautiful gift, Mark gazed upon his. Her dress was crumpled, her blonde locks were tousled and her mouth was beestung from their loving. Humbly he gave thanks for his good fortune that this woman was his.

'It's wonderful,' Emily at last managed to gasp.

'I wasn't sure whether you would prefer a different stone. I wasn't sure what Devlin got you.'

Emily looked into his eyes. 'A sapphire, and I gave it back without regret,' she said huskily. 'This is the most splendid gem I have ever seen.' She gazed up into his eyes. 'You'll never get it back.'

Mark drew forth the platinum shank from its satin nest and slid it on to her betrothal finger. 'I'd best marry you then…it cost a small fortune.' He placed a light reverential kiss on her scarlet lips. 'If you are still unsure what I think of you, Emily Beaumont, let me tell you in words,' he said huskily. 'I love and respect you utterly. I want us to be married by special licence tomorrow.' He smiled ruefully, 'And I would have told you that even had I not yet sampled what sweet advantages are to be had from taking a wanton bride…'